PENGUIN BOOKS
LAKSHADWEEP ADVENTURE

Deepak Dalal gave up a career in chemical engineering to write stories for children. He lives in Pune with his wife, two daughters and several dogs and cats. He enjoys wildlife, nature and the outdoors. His books include the Vikram–Aditya adventure series (for older readers) and the Feather Tales series (for younger readers). All his stories have a strong conservation theme.

Also by Deepak Dalal

The Vikram–Aditya Adventure Series (Penguin)
Ranthambore Adventure
Ladakh Adventure
Snow Leopard Adventure

Feather Tales Series (Puffin)
Talon the Falcon
A Flamingo in My Garden
The Paradise Flycatcher
The Golden Eagle

A
VIKRAM–ADITYA
STORY

LAKSHADWEEP
ADVENTURE

DEEPAK
DALAL

PENGUIN BOOKS
An imprint of Penguin Random House

PENGUIN BOOKS

USA | Canada | UK | Ireland | Australia
New Zealand | India | South Africa | China

Penguin Books is part of the Penguin Random House group of companies
whose addresses can be found at global.penguinrandomhouse.com

Published by Penguin Random House India Pvt. Ltd
7th Floor, Infinity Tower C, DLF Cyber City,
Gurgaon 122 002, Haryana, India

First published by Tarini Publishing 1998
Lakshadweep Adventure was published by Silverfish, an imprint of Grey Oak
Publishers, in association with Westland Publications Private Limited 2013
This edition published in Penguin Books by Penguin Random House India 2021

ISBN 9780143449447

Typeset in Adobe Caslon Pro by Manipal Technologies Limited, Manipal
Printed at Replika Press Pvt. Ltd, India

www.penguin.co.in

AUTHOR'S NOTE

Imagine that you are far from the mainland. Many hundreds of kilometres away. You are swimming in the deep blue sea, in 1000 metres of water. All at once, land rises from the depths that surround you. A dense and dazzlingly coloured underwater forest suddenly confronts you. The water is clear and fabulously transparent. The sun effortlessly penetrates to the seabed and you can see everything around you. There are fish everywhere. Little fish, big fish, brilliantly coloured fish. Turtles, sharks, snake-like eels, starfish, cowrie shells, clams. You have stumbled into a special world. It is the fascinating undersea world of a coral island.

There is something about coral islands that sets them apart from other islands. These islands are surrounded by coral reefs. Inside the reef there exists a calm, transparent body of water called a lagoon. Outside, the sea is choppy and deep. Within the lagoon, you float in perhaps 5 or 10 metres of water, but outside, a little distance from the reef, you could be floating in 1000 metres of water! Coral islands have wonderful beaches of white sand. This sand is not the same as that found on beaches along the mainland coast. This is coral sand.

India does have its very own coral islands—the Lakshadweep Islands. They are located in the Arabian Sea and run parallel to the western coast (a note on the origin of coral islands is given at the end of the book). Starting 300 kilometres west of the southern state of Kerala, they progress in the form of a broken chain all the way down to Sri Lanka and beyond. The upper section of this island chain is called Lakshadweep and belongs to India. The lower section is called the Maldives.

The people of the Lakshadweep Islands are warm and friendly. Fishing is their livelihood and many of them are great sailors. Visiting the islands is always a treat. There is much for tourists to enjoy—coconut palms, wonderful beaches and transparent lagoons that are perfect for water sports like windsurfing, sailing and snorkelling. But the appeal of Lakshadweep is not just the wind, sand and stars. The most bewitching attraction of them all is its coral—the reefs and their myriad creatures.

KADMAT

The Lakshadweep Islands.

Vikram googled the islands on the internet the moment his father permitted him to join his friend Aditya on holiday there.

There were thirty-six islands, he discovered. They lay far out in the Arabian Sea, some 300 kilometres west of the port of Kochi, in Kerala. You had to travel overnight on a boat from Kochi to get there. Or if you were willing to pay, you could travel by plane, or even helicopter. Aditya's dad, Captain Abbas Khan, was a naval helicopter pilot based at Kadmat, one of the bigger islands of the Lakshadweep archipelago.

Vikram already knew that the islands were coral atolls. His father, an ecologist and a wildlife lover, had told him that coral reefs harboured so many different fish, corals and other creatures that when it came to biodiversity, they were second only to tropical rainforests.

'The islands with their coconut palms and their beaches are magnificent,' he had told Vikram on the phone. 'A fabulous vista of sand and sea. But . . .' Vikram's dad took a long pause. '. . . but that's only part of the story. A tiny part if you ask me.' He paused again. 'If you're looking for the real treasure of the islands, dive underwater. You will enter a different world when you do so. A world unlike anything you have ever seen. It's down under that you'll find the hidden soul of the islands. Their beauty and charm is all underwater.' He had gone on about scuba diving and turtles and fish and sharks and corals. Vikram had listened spellbound.

With enthusiasm matching Vikram's father's, Aditya had raved about windsurfing. 'It's the most elemental and enjoyable form of sailing, Vikram! The equipment is just a board and a sail,' he said. 'That's it . . . nothing more.' To get moving, all that was needed was wind. A decent wind would fill the sail and the board would move forward. Of course, windsurfing wasn't as simple as that. The sport was hard to learn, he had warned, but once you got a hang of the basics, it was the most exhilarating way to sail.

Vikram and Aditya studied at a boarding school in the Nilgiris. The term was nearing its end. Although the days slipped by quickly, their passage was much too slow for Vikram. Finally, their exams were done and it was time for the winter holidays. A taxi collected the boys from their school the next morning and a long drive on winding roads brought them to the port of Kochi, where they arrived in time to board a boat sailing overnight to the islands. The next morning was bright and clear and when Vikram awoke and looked out of his cabin window, he set eyes on a panorama even more beautiful than what his father had described.

An island hovered before him, floating in a sea that was blue and turquoise and fabulously transparent. It was long and mostly green, fringed by a forest of palm trees. Sandwiched between the trees and the sea was a strip of sand, more white than brown, and it stretched as far as Vikram could see.

Kadmat Island.

Vikram's heart leapt. The island was everything his father had said, and more.

A boy named Faisal was waiting for them on the Kadmat jetty when they disembarked from their boat. Aditya's father had flown away on duty that morning, and had requested Faisal to help the boys in his absence. Faisal's father, Mr Mohammed Koya, was a great friend of Captain Khan, and since Faisal's school was shut for the holidays, he had made himself available.

Faisal was short with wavy hair, and his face was smooth and baby-like. Like most islanders, his skin was dark, but what set him apart was the permanent twinkle in his eyes. Faisal loved the sea and he was exceptionally good at all water sports, which was no wonder since his father was the head of the water sports centre in Kadmat.

The boys hit it off from the moment they met. Within an hour of their arrival, they had swum out into the sea. Later, they collected windsurf boards from the water sports centre and Vikram watched enviously as Aditya and Faisal sailed out far into the lagoon.

Vikram spent the next few days teaching himself windsurfing. As Aditya had told him, the learning was the

7

hardest part of the sport. The simple act of standing on a board in constantly moving water was difficult. Every time Vikram stood, the board would rock and he would fall. When finally he could balance, he worked on the sail, pulling it out of the water. But the moment the sail emerged, it would catch the wind and fling him back into the sea. Aditya and Faisal, if they were watching, would laugh, and Vikram would laugh along with them. Although he swallowed litres of seawater with his numerous falls, Vikram was sporting enough to see the comical side of his inept performances. In spite of the pain and exhaustion, Vikram persevered and eventually, after endless hours of hard work, he managed to sail the board.

Vikram's achievements were amateurish at best, but he had gained enough confidence to leave the shore and follow Faisal and Aditya into deeper waters. Kadmat Island, in the manner of all coral atolls, is surrounded by a huge body of shallow, calm water called a lagoon. The lagoon itself is bordered by a coral reef and one morning, Faisal and Aditya escorted Vikram to the reef.

'See that line of white?' said Faisal as they drew near. 'That's the coral reef.'

An undulating band of froth stretched on either side of them. The foam and froth were waves. Back near the shore, there were hardly any waves, but out here, at the very edge of the lagoon, there were plenty.

The boys dropped their sails well short of the waves. The water was distinctly choppy here and Vikram found it hard to stand on his swaying board.

'Look down,' said Faisal, 'at the water we are floating on. It's coloured turquoise, isn't it?'

'Turquoise it is,' said Aditya. 'But more green than blue if you ask me.'

Faisal nodded. 'That's right. More green than blue. But it's a very light green, and that's because the water here—in the lagoon—is shallow.' Faisal then pointed at the coral reef. 'Now look out across the reef, at the open sea beyond. The water is a dark blue there.'

'Really dark,' said Vikram. 'A kind of inky blue.'

'And why is the blue so dark?' asked Faisal. He looked questioningly at his friends. 'Anybody?'

Vikram gazed at the deep blue sea. The water there was restless. It was heaving and the swells were tipped white. 'The dark colour is because the sea is deep there,' he said.

'How did you know that?' asked Faisal.

Aditya laughed. 'You aren't Vikram's classmate, so you don't know stuff about him. He's the sort that researches everything. You won't believe it, but back at school when teachers would forget something, they'd ask him. Your question about the colour of the water—' Aditya waved a hand, 'it's elementary for our dear Vikram.'

Vikram laughed. 'Don't believe a word Aditya says. I care to read. Aditya doesn't. That's the difference.'

Faisal stared at Vikram. 'So then if you've researched the islands, why don't you tell us what you've read?'

'Fascinating stuff actually,' said Vikram. 'Particularly about your coral reefs. They say that the coral reef is the dividing line between the lagoon and the open sea. I read

9

that the water in the lagoon is mostly shallow.' Vikram looked down, peering at the sand beneath. 'It is shallow here, about 10–15 feet deep,' he estimated. 'But if we cross that white line that marks the coral reef, it's the equivalent of swimming off the edge of a mountain. That dark water ahead is some 5–10,000 feet deep. It's hard to take in, isn't it? I mean, here we are, in some 20-foot-deep water, but just there, across the reef, the water is *5000* feet deep. I didn't believe this when I read about it. But I can see it now. The colour of the water is a giveaway. Light green where it is shallow, and dark blue where it is deep.'

Aditya's eyes lit up. 'That's wild. Why don't we sail out there? Let's take our boards across the coral reef, off the edge as Vikram says, and into the deep sea.'

Faisal shook his head. 'Uh-huh. Can't do that. We have to stay inside the lagoon. Dad's instructions. No crossing the coral reef into the open sea. We break his rules and he will confiscate our boards. You know my father. He's a shark when it comes to rules. He bites if you don't obey them.'

Vikram and Aditya could vouch for Mr Mohammed Koya's rigidity. Faisal's father was a short man of slight build, his dark face identical to Faisal's except that he had a moustache and his hair was thinning at the sides. At first sight he seemed mild-mannered, but his calm demeanour masked an iron will and an uncompromising attitude when it came to rules.

Mr Koya wasn't the kind of person who held back his anger. If shortcuts were taken or things weren't done the way they were supposed to, he didn't hesitate to punish those involved. Aditya, whose disdain for discipline was legendary back at his school, had fallen foul of Mr Koya on their very first interaction.

Mr Koya was a certified scuba-diving instructor and he had volunteered to teach the boys. For Vikram, diving and the underwater exploration of Kadmat was without a doubt the highlight of his holiday, and he had trembled with anticipation when they had first ventured out into the lagoon with Mr Koya. The boys had listened raptly while Mr Koya had held up a scuba suit and painstakingly explained its various parts and controls. But when Mr Koya had switched to the subject of safety, Aditya's interest had dwindled.

When compared with other activities, scuba diving stands out as a pursuit where safety is of paramount importance. If things go wrong underwater—for example, the misfortune of a tank running out of air or a diver losing his mouthpiece—the consequences can be fatal. So every instructor explains safety routines in great length and detail.

Even on the best of days, Aditya had scant regard for safety procedures. But on that morning, with a scuba-diving suit strapped to his body for the first time in his life, he paid no attention to Mr Koya. This might have been overlooked, but Aditya made things even worse by diving underwater while Mr Koya was talking. Naturally, Mr Koya hadn't taken kindly to this. He had ordered Aditya out of the water and put an end to the classes for both the boys.

He had relented only when Captain Khan had persuaded him to resume their training. Aditya had been at his best behaviour since, hanging on to every word Mr Koya spoke, and participating enthusiastically in safety drills.

Vikram's introduction to the undersea realm of a coral island was the most fascinating experience of his stay at Kadmat. A new world opened its watery doors to him. Earlier, he couldn't stay underwater any longer than his breath permitted him. But the air tank strapped on his back eliminated the handicap, doing away with the compulsion to return to the surface. He could stay under as long as he wanted and this empowered him with an incredible sense of freedom.

For as long as Vikram could remember, he had wanted to experience the underwater world the way a fish does. He desired to hear the sounds they heard, breathe underwater the way they did, see exactly what they saw and travel alongside them. Now, finally, he could.

The first thing that struck him was that all underwater sounds were magnified, as if a sub-aquatic volume knob had been cranked high. The whisper of water moving across the sand—he could never have dreamt that it would be so loud. Even the fish, they made distinct watery noises that he could hear from far. He could hear the waves in the distance too as they broke on the coral reef.

The fish fascinated Vikram. Some were as long as his arm, others smaller even than his fingers. Some swam individually, some in pairs and several sought shelter in numbers, schooling in large shoals. The fish didn't mind him swimming alongside them, but if he drew near, they would edge away.

Other than fish, there wasn't much else to see along the shoreline. The area was mostly sandy, blotched here and there by drifts of seagrass. There was hardly any coral and this disappointed the boys.

Faisal consoled his friends. That was how it was in the lagoon, he said, fun for a while, but boring afterwards. According to him, they were wasting their time in the lagoon, especially when the coral reef with its promise of beauty and adventure was so tantalizingly near. He entranced Vikram and Aditya with vivid descriptions of his dives along the coral reef, so much so that the boys entreated Mr Koya, begging permission to swim out to the reef.

Mr Koya had refused outright. 'Not a chance,' he said. 'Diving isn't only about fun. There's a safety aspect also. You boys might think you are ready for the reef, but you aren't. There's a lot you have to learn before I take you there.' He gave the boys a knowing look. 'I know that it's my son who is instigating you. He's getting bored in the lagoon, and I understand that. Faisal has sold you a dream about Kadmat's coral reef, and he is absolutely right. The reef is a fascinating place. You can explore the entire island and I guarantee you that you won't find anything that comes close to its beauty. Sure, I'll take you to the reef, but you will have to learn every last thing about your equipment and you will have to practise safety procedures over and over again before I do.'

The days had quickly flashed by. Mornings were spent with Mr Koya in the lagoon, and in the evenings, they sailed their windsurf boards. Sometimes they toured the island on bicycles. Kadmat Island was thin and long and exceptionally beautiful. There was hardly a square metre on the island that wasn't shaded by a canopy of palm fronds. And at the verge of the palm forest, where the trees slanted to the sea, a beach filled with powdery white sand began—a beach that encircled the entire island.

Sometimes Vikram wondered if he was dreaming. He could never have imagined that a holiday could be so enjoyable, and he often feared this feeling wouldn't last. But wasn't that the way with all good things? However much you didn't want them to, didn't they always come to an end? Unfortunately for Vikram, his misgivings were about to come true. Events were conspiring against them, bringing to an end their joyful stay at Kadmat.

It was Captain Khan who broke the news to them.

Aditya's father was a tall, well-built man. He sported a beard that was completely white. This contrasted with his full head of dark hair flecked only here and there with streaks of white. He was an energetic man who was happiest when he was bustling around and doing things. Although Vikram had spent two weeks in the islands, besides exchanging pleasantries, he had hardly spent any time with Captain Khan. The officer had been in and out of Kadmat, called away on duty.

After a week at Kochi, Captain Khan had returned to Kadmat. Although he had flown in late in the afternoon, in his usual frenetic manner he had organized an evening barbecue on the beach for the boys and his friend Mr Mohammed Koya.

Captain Khan had dispatched the boys to the market to buy tuna. When they returned, he had dressed and cooked the fish. Captain Khan was an excellent chef, and the boys and Mr Koya had expressed their appreciation in the most rewarding way possible—a simple yet significant silence during their meal.

When they were done, Vikram and Aditya lay down on the sand and stared sightlessly at the sky. There was no moon, but the black of the night was hidden behind a patchwork of stars. A breeze was blowing over the lagoon, sweeping across the island, stirring the palms overhead.

Aditya stretched and yawned. 'Oh man,' he said. 'This is the life.'

Mr Koya smiled. 'Here on these islands, we are blessed with an abundance of the sun, the sand and the stars. That's what draws people here.'

Captain Khan leaned back on his elbows. 'I hear you've been driving the boys hard in your scuba sessions, Mohammed.'

Mr Koya grinned. 'Who told you?' he asked.

'Guess,' replied Captain Khan.

'Can't be Vikram,' he said. 'He's not the complaining sort. Has to be Aditya.'

Captain Khan laughed.

'That's not true,' protested Aditya. 'I never complained about the lessons and practice. It's about the reef. I want to go out and dive there.'

'That's right,' Vikram piped in. 'We've done the drills so often that we know them by heart. We are ready for the reef.'

Faisal backed his friends. 'I agree with Vikram, Papa. I've been watching them. They are ready.'

Captain Khan turned to Mr Koya. 'You might have to fast-track your diving programme for the boys, Mohammed. I have some news and it isn't good.'

Mr Koya sat up. 'It's true then,' he said. 'People have been talking, but I thought it was a rumour.'

Captain Khan's face turned grave. 'It's true. The information is still classified and I shouldn't be speaking about it, but the story will be out tomorrow. So you might as well hear it from me.' He paused, his eyes flashing in the starlight as he looked at each of the boys. 'Kadmat Island will be closing down soon.'

'Eh?' said Aditya. 'What do you mean, closing down?'

'You've seen the presidential huts at the south end of the island, haven't you?'

Aditya stared at his dad, puzzled. 'Yes, we go there often. But what's that got to do with closing down Kadmat?'

Vikram remembered the huts. The sunsets from there were exceptionally beautiful.

'The huts are going to be occupied soon,' said Captain Khan.

'So?' said Aditya. 'What's that got to do with us?'

'The place is going to be taken over by the Indian Navy. They will be bringing a guest there. A special guest. He is a Tamilian from Sri Lanka, and his life is in danger. The man has fallen foul of the Sri Lankan militants. They have sworn to kill him and they almost did. It was in the papers and on TV a few weeks ago. They attacked him in Chennai, but he managed to escape. He's what you might call a "high-security" risk and Chennai's police force felt they could not guarantee his safety. He is being brought here to Kadmat for protection.'

'Why Kadmat?' exclaimed Vikram.

'I'll answer that, Abbas,' said Mr Koya. 'This kind of thing has happened before. "High-security" guests are often brought to the Lakshadweep Islands. Because of their remoteness, it's impossible for anyone to come here undetected. In addition, we have a large naval outpost here. It is very easy for the navy to seal off an island . . . and they do an excellent job. "High-security" guests are safe here and that's why they bring them to Kadmat. Let's look at it another way for a moment. Let's suppose that the militants manage to break through the security cordon and capture the guest. The question is, what next? Where do they go from here? We are surrounded by the sea. There is no place to hide. The navy can hunt down the enemy in no time at all. So from a strategic point of view, our islands are a great place for sheltering these kinds of guests.'

'Huh,' said Aditya. 'I never thought of it that way. But I still don't understand. What's the bad news? So what if the navy seals off the presidential huts? They are at the tip of the island and we hardly go there.'

Mr Koya shook his head. 'The navy takes no chances. The entire lagoon will be sealed off.'

'It means that there will be no windsurfing, no scuba diving, no sailing and no swimming,' said Faisal.

Aditya stared in shock. 'You're joking, Faisal,' he said.

Mr Koya shook his head. 'Faisal isn't joking. He's right. The lagoon will be out of bounds.'

Vikram's heart sank. The lagoon, the sea and the reef—they couldn't venture there any more. The soul of the island was underwater. That was what his father had said. What good was the island if its soul was locked away?

Mr Koya looked at the boys. Aditya's face seemed to have shrunk. Vikram's shoulders were drooping and his head was down. He made a clucking sound. 'Your holiday isn't ruined,' he said. 'I know of a way to save it.'

Captain Khan raised his eyebrows. 'How?' he asked.

'This rumour of Kadmat being sealed off has been around for several days now. I didn't pay much attention to it, but I did think of the boys and how disappointed they would be. It struck me then that Kadmat isn't the only island with a lagoon. My brother, Faisal's uncle, lives on Kalpeni Island. It is a nice place with a lagoon as big and as beautiful as Kadmat's, and there's a water sports centre there too. A colleague of mine runs it and he will be glad to supply you with whatever equipment you need.'

'Do they have windsurf boards?' asked Aditya. His head was up and he was staring at Mr Koya.

'Many,' replied Mr Koya.

'Wow!' Aditya's face lit up.

Captain Khan clapped his friend on the shoulder. 'Great idea, Mohammed. I can fly the boys there, and they can stay with your brother.'

'Sure,' said Mr Koya. 'He will look after them. This works out well for Faisal too. He hasn't visited his uncle in a long time.'

Vikram turned to look at Faisal and did a double take when he saw the sullen expression on his face.

Captain Khan noticed Faisal's downcast look too. 'What's the matter?' he asked. 'You don't seem too pleased with the Kalpeni plan.'

'My son doesn't like his uncle,' explained Mr Koya. He placed an arm around Faisal's shoulders. 'You have your friends along this time. It won't be so bad.'

'I'm not going,' said Faisal. His face was set and the twinkle was absent from his eyes. 'Vikram and Aditya can go if they like. I'm staying here.'

'You must go, Faisal.' Mr Koya's tone was firm. 'Family is important to us. You have to understand that. Basheer may have his flaws, but he is your uncle. You can choose to accompany your friends now or visit him alone later. I'm sure you will prefer going with your friends. And I'll make it more fun for you. I will arrange for a boat, so you can all go on a fishing trip. How about that?'

Vikram and Aditya looked at one another.

'Mohammed Uncle, you are the best!' exclaimed Aditya. He pushed Faisal playfully. 'Stop sulking, you nit. We'll all be together. You won't have to spend much time with your uncle. We'll be windsurfing, fishing, sailing or whatever. We'll have hundreds of things to do. We'll have a great time.'

Faisal turned away and stared moodily out at the lagoon.

His father patted his back. 'That's settled then,' he said. 'I'll call my brother.'

'Sounds great,' said Vikram. 'Mr Koya, do they have scuba-diving facilities there?'

Mr Koya shook his head, 'I'm afraid not.' Then he smiled. 'Since you boys are going away, I'll be extra nice. I'll take you scuba diving to the reef tomorrow as a farewell present.'

THE REEF

It was nine o'clock in the morning.

The sun was shining mercilessly from a pale blue sky. Sweat moistened Vikram's brow as he and Aditya shouldered heavy air tanks across the sand to a motorboat anchored at the edge of the beach. A bright blue sunroof covered the deck area of the boat and at its aft end, there was an upraised platform and a navigation wheel.

Soon the hull of the boat was buried beneath a tangle of masks, flippers, buoyancy vests, air cylinders and assorted diving equipment. Mr Koya and Faisal then rearranged the gear into sets, one for each person.

When the sorting was completed, Mr Koya gathered everybody beneath the shade of a palm tree.

He turned to Vikram and Aditya. 'Excited?' he asked.

'I can tell you Aditya is,' Captain Khan said. 'My son gets that big grin on his face when he is all charged up—a lot like Rusty before his morning walk.'

Aditya didn't take kindly to his father's analogy. 'Thanks, Dad. Like our dog, huh? Shouldn't I be jumping everywhere then and knocking stuff over the way Rusty does?'

Everyone laughed.

'And you, Vikram?' asked Mr Koya.

Captain Khan spoke up again, 'Vikram is different. I can assure you that he's as pumped up as Aditya, but he doesn't show it. He holds these things inside.'

It was true. Vikram's face was expressionless. Meanwhile, Aditya's excitement was so evident that he looked in danger of drooling like Rusty at any moment.

'If it were my first time,' said Mr Koya, 'my heart would be thumping as hard as those waves battering the reef. There's nothing that can prepare you for the experience of a coral reef. It's a world like you've never seen before.'

Mr Koya paused. The smile exited his face. His tone turned crisp and businesslike. 'But there are rules we have to observe when underwater. You've learnt them in the lagoon, but we're going to go over them once more. Faisal and Abbas have dived often and know what to expect. You boys are first-timers. So you better listen because it's mainly for you that I am going through our routine once more. If you don't understand anything I say, speak up now. Because later on, when we are underwater we won't be able to talk to one another, and I will not be able to explain things.

'The most important aspect of scuba diving is that it is a team operation. We will stay together and move in a proper planned manner.' Mr Koya drilled Aditya with his gaze. 'Your father tells me you have a mind of your own. That doesn't work here. We are going down as a team. Anyone who indulges in individual heroics can endanger an entire diving group. You will follow me and do exactly as I do, is that clear?'

'Yes, sir!' Aditya's reply was so military-like that Vikram half-expected his friend to raise his hand in a salute.

Aditya's firm response satisfied Mr Koya. 'Right,' he said. 'I'm going to start with the signals. As you know, the only way we can communicate underwater is through the sign language I have taught you. I'd like to review those signals.'

They practised the signals. Mr Koya started with the one that indicated the diver wasn't feeling good, then continued with the action, which warned that the diver was running out of air, then the OK signal, direction signals and many others.

'So that's taken care of,' said Mr Koya when they were done. 'Now let's review the things we will do out at sea, before we enter the water. First, I will select a spot and drop anchor. We will then strap on our diving gear. I will check each one of you before you enter the water. When I give you the okay, we will swim to the anchor rope and work our way underwater holding the rope. Once you are down on the seabed, gather around the anchor. There will be a final equipment check before we set off. When I give the signal to start swimming, we will do so in an ordered manner. I will be in the lead, Vikram and Faisal will be next, followed by Aditya. You, Abbas, will be last. Got that?'

'Yes, sir,' replied Vikram and Aditya together.

A smile flitted on Mr Koya's face. 'Good,' he said. 'You boys are going to experience a different kind of sea today. We will be exiting the lagoon and diving on the seaward side of the reef. That's out in the ocean where the water runs deep and it can be a lot rougher. Swimming gets a little more challenging and you should be prepared. My personal experience is that it's easier to swim underwater than along the surface.'

It was cool under the palm tree. The sweat had evaporated from Vikram's brow. Faisal had departed to perform last-minute checks on the engine. The others listened intently to Mr Koya.

'We will be swimming at a depth of 30–40 feet along the reef. You will be surrounded by coral and thousands of fish. Although you will see a lot of wonderful things, don't touch them. I might pick up the odd coral or fish for you to see. You can touch these but nothing else. Remember, the ocean belongs to the creatures who live there. We must be courteous and show respect for them and their property in exactly the same manner you would expect a guest at your home to behave. We might even come across reef sharks, as they are fairly common in the area.'

Vikram felt a delicious chill run through him. He glanced at Aditya who grinned at him.

'You don't have to worry about reef sharks because they aren't the man-eating variety that you see in the movies. Luckily, those killer sharks—the great whites—aren't found in our waters. Our reef sharks are peaceful, but it doesn't mean that you can misbehave with them. When provoked, they can kill with a single bite. For that matter, almost any big fish can seriously injure you. I need you to understand that.' Mr Koya shifted his gaze from Aditya to Vikram and back. 'Is that clear?' he asked.

'Yes, sir,' said the boys.

'Right, then,' said Mr Koya. 'It's time to go!'

They boarded the motorboat and cast off. They cut through the calm lagoon waters, making for the distant white line that marked the reef.

At Kadmat, like at all other coral islands, at the edge of the lagoon rises a sharp wall of coral that encircles the island and shelters it from the powerful waves of the open seas. The coral safeguards the island, shielding it from the sea. If there is no coral to hold back the waves, over time the sea will sweep the island away. The coral prevents this by absorbing the force of the waves and keeping the sea out. But the coral also forms a barrier, blocking passage when travelling from the island to the sea. Boats require a certain amount of free water below them for safe passage. The coral reef ascends all the way to the surface, providing no clearance at all. Coral, which is as hard as stone, rips apart the underside of any boat that foolishly attempts to cross. But there are stretches where the reef is submerged deep enough to provide a safe passage for boats to enter and exit. These channels are marked by lighthouses, buoys or poles.

The lagoon waters were calm as they chugged towards the lighthouses that marked one of Kadmat's two exit channels. But the placid conditions changed as they drew near the lighthouses. Very quickly, the water lost its smooth, tabletop appearance. It started to heave, rearing and plunging in a turbulent manner. The boat rocked alarmingly as waves smashed against it, drenching everyone with their spray.

Although Faisal had warned Vikram, he wasn't prepared for the raw power of the waves of the exit channel.

'Hold on tight, here comes the first big one,' shouted Mr Koya as he guided the boat into the open sea. The roar of the surf reverberated in their ears. Vikram watched a frothing wall of water move swiftly towards them.

'Yoo-hoo!' shouted Faisal as they took the wave head-on, rising over it and splashing down on the other side. Mr Koya quickly straightened the boat as the next wave rolled towards them. This time Vikram, Aditya and Faisal all shouted in unison as they rose triumphantly above it and on towards the next one. The waves soon diminished in size and Mr Koya steered away from them. Selecting a calm section of water not far from the frothing line that marked the reef, he cut the boat's engine.

'Your diving gear,' shouted Mr Koya, busying himself with the anchor. 'Get yourselves ready.'

The rocking motion of the boat made it difficult for them to slip their gear on. After a period of huffing, tugging and fumbling, they were ready. Mr Koya checked everyone's equipment before waving them into the water.

Vikram grinned at Aditya who winked back at him.

'I'm going in first,' said Aditya. He sat on the edge of the boat and somersaulted backwards into the water. Vikram squatted next on the railing. Clasping his mask to his face, he flipped himself into the blue waters of the Arabian Sea.

The first thing that struck Vikram was the coolness of the water. Tasting salt, he adjusted his mask and mouthpiece. When he drew a breath, air rushed into his lungs. Satisfied with his equipment, he paddled to the anchor rope. The rope pulled and tugged when he held it, twitching as if it had a life of its own. Vikram tingled with excitement as he made his way down. It was happening. Yes! He was entering the undersea world of a coral island.

Surface sounds quickly faded, overpowered by those of the watery expanse around him. Most pervasive was the underwater wash of the waves as they surged against the reef. Surprisingly, their boat—floating far above—contributed volubly to the din as it groaned and strained at the anchor rope. His mouthpiece was noisy too. It hissed every time Vikram sucked air, and bubbles fizzed and erupted when he exhaled.

As Vikram swam downwards, the additional weight of the water above him disturbed his ears. Mr Koya had taught them how to rid themselves of this funny feeling by holding their noses and blowing till their ears popped. This action equalized the pressure in their ears with that of the water above them. They had been warned to continuously equalize, failing which they could contract severe headaches later on.

Down on the seabed, it seemed as if the whole world was in motion. Nothing was stationary—not the boat above, not the rope, not the blades of seagrass below. Everything swayed with the restless motion of the sea. Visibility was excellent. The sun shone unhindered from above, it's light spearing through the water as if it wasn't there. Although there was coral on the seabed, it was the fish that drew Vikram's attention. They were everywhere—above him, below him, floating by his side. They all seemed to be staring at him, inspecting him in a mild yet inquisitive manner. They made no attempt to move away, nor did they bother to come closer.

Vikram was so fascinated by them that he did not notice his hand being tugged. He was suddenly twirled around and he found himself staring at Mr Koya who was gazing intently at him, as if asking if anything was wrong. He pulled Vikram with him to where the others were floating. Faisal and Aditya swam towards Vikram, signalling the OK sign. Vikram connected his thumb and forefinger too, letting them know that he was OK.

Mr Koya then ran a final check on their equipment. Satisfied, he exchanged the OK signal with each of them. He then beckoned Vikram and Faisal to follow him, next was Aditya and Captain Khan brought up the rear.

Although Vikram was a good swimmer, he struggled to keep up with Mr Koya. The conditions in the sea were different from what they had encountered in the lagoon. Here the water moved continuously, exerting an invisible, shifting pressure. Every time he moved one way, the current seemed to tug him in another. He was forced to kick hard. He discovered that his flippers were extremely useful for coping with the current.

They swam downwards, along the sloping edge of the reef. Mr Koya raised a hand, pointing. In front—stretching across their path like a live curtain—was a shoal of pale blue fish, each no bigger than Vikram's little finger. There must have been hundreds upon hundreds of them. As they approached, the shoal turned in one flickering movement, their bodies glinting briefly in the sunlight, and darted out of their path.

Now, after all those hours spent snorkelling with Faisal, Vikram could identify several of the fish around him. On one side, there was a group of big striped fish, each one half as tall as Vikram. They had odd mouths with pouted lips, and Vikram smiled as he recalled their name: sweetlips. The finger-sized fish that had moved out of their path were called blue pullers. The iridescent green ones pecking at the coral were parrotfish. Vikram spotted a shoal of large fish with bumped heads. These were batfish, and each one was as big as his chest. Multicoloured butterfly fish with Pinocchio-like snouts swam serenely through the coral. There were so many fish that Vikram found it hard to keep track of them. Above, they floated in large shoals, and below, dropping away into the depths, Vikram could see many hundreds more—some darting busily here and there, others drifting with the currents.

Mr Koya pulled up suddenly. Raising a hand, he pointed at what appeared to be a cavity in the coral. Faisal grabbed Vikram and Aditya by their arms, holding them back. Vikram soon saw why. A long fish with a snake-like body swayed sinuously above the cavity, its body half inside the hole. It had a dark, large head and a hideous mouth spiked with sharp teeth, which it opened and closed as it stared at them.

A moray eel.

Mr Koya had told them that these snake-like fish lived in cracks and holes in the coral. They are active mostly at night when they come out to hunt. They rarely attacked, but if provoked, their bites could cause serious injuries.

As they swam away, the eel backed into its den leaving only its head and mouth visible.

A short while later, Mr Koya stopped once more and scooped up a fragile creature clinging to an outcrop of coral. Shaped like a starfish, it had small purple-coloured tentacles. It was tiny enough to fit into the palm of Mr Koya's hand. Vikram and Aditya stroked the little tentacles before Mr Koya gently replaced it where he had found it. Further on, Mr Koya reached out for a cucumber-shaped object half-buried in the sand—a sea cucumber. Holding it, he squeezed gently. Out trickled a fine, white substance that floated in the water. Vikram tried to catch the wispy strands. Faisal grabbed his hand, restraining him, but it was too late. The milky material wrapped stickily around his fingers and try as he might, Vikram could not shake it loose. Faisal appeared to be laughing behind his mask. He waved Vikram onward, his body language suggesting that Vikram give up trying to remove the sticky material.

Vikram marvelled at the coral as they swam forward. Left to itself, the reef wall would have been drab and colourless. But the coral changed all that. The organisms crowded the reef wall as far as Vikram could see, weaving a tapestry of other-worldly beauty. They were present in all shapes and sizes. Some resembled mushrooms, some were flat and wide, some were round and textured and many were prickly, like cactus stalks. What was even more startling was the bewildering range of colours they flaunted: sizzling yellows, blazing browns, radiant purples, fiery reds and dazzling greens.

Vikram spotted a sea turtle. It was swimming below them and was eyeing them suspiciously. The reptiles are bulky and awkward on land, but here in the water, the turtle floated ever so gracefully, occasionally shifting its flippers to counter the currents. The rest of the team had seen the turtle too and Mr Koya was signalling for them to swim towards it. The reptile turned and paddled away. They followed, admiring the humped shell encasing the animal's body.

Aditya, who was lagging behind, noticed movement to one side and turned. Some distance away was another turtle, bigger than the one the others were following. Deciding that he preferred the second turtle, Aditya changed course and swam towards it.

Aditya marvelled at the size of the turtle as he approached it. The creature had cocked its head and was eyeing Aditya. It allowed him to come close before paddling away. Aditya followed, trying to draw closer, but the turtle stayed comfortably ahead of him. Aditya swam on, oblivious to the fact that he was moving away from his group. Suddenly, in a flurry of flippers, the turtle shot away, leaving a peeved Aditya no chance to follow.

Aditya halted and looked back the way he had come. The water was crystal clear, allowing for good visibility. He could faintly see a mass of air bubbles in the distance and he paddled leisurely in their direction. Below him, fronds of seagrass swayed in the currents. Two large fish floated idly in front of him. Their outlines were familiar. He had seen them before. Aditya froze, coming to an abrupt halt.

Sharks!

SHARKS

The first thing that struck Aditya was that he was alone. He could see his group in the distance, but the sharks were directly in his path, blocking his route to them. Aditya's throat turned dry. A prickly feeling spread inside, as if he had swallowed a fistful of sand. His heart thumped so powerfully that all he heard was its frantic beating.

What a fool he had been. If only he had remained with the group. Now he couldn't get back. The sharks were in the way. The best he could do was manoeuvre to one side and hope to steal away from them.

He turned slowly, watching the sharks. They made no attempt to follow. Taking his eyes off them, he looked ahead. Aditya froze once more, quivering to a halt. A numbness spread inside him. Swimming slowly towards him was another shark.

This shark was bigger than the other two. Its mouth was a slash on its underside. The teeth inside flashed in the underwater light. The eyes set in the upper part of its head were cold and unfeeling. Its grey skin rippled as it swam towards him.

Aditya breathed deeply, struggling to control his panic.

He looked back. The first two sharks were still there. Aditya turned towards them. His best hope was to make it back to his group. It didn't matter that the shark pair blocked his path. He would swim towards them. Not exactly at them, but to their left, so as to bypass them and make a dash for his group.

The solitary shark behind was still swimming towards him.

Forget about that one, he told himself. *Focus on the other two.*

Blood pounded in Aditya's ears. His body had started to shake. He clenched his fists. *Calm down*, he ordered himself. *Take it easy. Relax.*

He looked at the shark pair and his heart skipped a beat. They weren't stationary any more. They were moving, swishing their tail fins. The course they had set appeared to intersect his, thwarting his attempt to squeeze past them.

Aditya shut his eyes. Fright and despair were clouding his mind. He had to get a grip on himself. He drew deeply on his breathing pipe. His wits, his pluck, his determination—where were they? Reaching deep inside himself, he gathered the crumbled remnants of his will. Working doggedly, he expelled the fear that had seized him. His brain started to clear. His ability to reason asserted itself. *These were reef sharks,* he told himself. *They would not attack him.* Wasn't that what Mr Koya had said? By nature, Aditya was a brave boy. His decisions were typically of the bold variety, particularly when made under conditions of duress and pressure. Stuck between the sharks, he decided not to turn away from them. He would do the opposite instead. He would swim directly at them.

Aditya kicked hard with his flippers. The sharks moved forward. They held their bearing, coming straight at him. Closer and closer they came. He saw the vertical slits that were their gills. *This is it*, Aditya told himself. *It's all or nothing now.* He increased his speed. The sharks paused, watching through their cold eyes. Aditya swam straight on. When he was near enough to reach out and touch them, they moved apart. Then, with a powerful flick of their tails, they surged forward.

Aditya had no time to think. The force of their sudden movement created a powerful current, which catapulted him head over heels. Aditya's mask was torn from his face and his breathing pipe slipped from his mouth. Saltwater blurred his eyes, severely limiting his vision. He lost all sense of direction; he could not tell which way was up and which was down. He groped blindly for his breathing pipe but failed to locate it. Where were the sharks? The breathing pipe had to be within reach, but try as he might, he could not locate it. He decided to surface, but which way was up? His chest tightened from lack of air. He opened his mouth and gagged as it filled with seawater. His head was on fire; he felt as if his chest was collapsing within him.

Something clasped his hand and pulled him with a strong jerk. Aditya was too far gone to resist. A hissing object was forced into his mouth. Aditya fought, trying to wrench it away but despite his struggles, it remained, emitting a stream of bubbles. His breathing pipe! He drew heavily on it, but to his horror, water entered his mouth. Breathe out, he recalled, you have to breathe out before taking your first breath. Aditya summoned his last reserves, forcing his oxygen-starved chest outwards and then pulled hard on the pipe. Cool, heady, life-saving air rushed into his lungs. Aditya breathed long and hard, sucking greedily at the tube.

His mind slowly stabilized. His wrist. Something was clamping it hard. He shook it, trying to free himself, but whatever it was only tightened its grip. He turned. A blurred shadow was floating in front of him, he felt rather than saw it pushing something into his hand.

His mask!

Aditya slipped it on and cleared it. His surroundings sprang into focus. Mr Koya was staring at him, his expression a mix of concern and anger.

Mr Koya cupped his fingers in the OK signal. Aditya cupped his fingers too, signalling he was all right. Mr Koya held on to Aditya while the rest of the group— still some distance away—swam towards them. Of the sharks there was no sign. Aditya wondered what had happened to them. He shuddered, recalling the moment they had lunged forward. He shook uncontrollably. The diving instructor tightened his grip, preventing Aditya from floating away.

The group arrived in a flurry of bubbles, their worried expressions visible through their masks. Captain Khan grabbed Aditya, but Mr Koya motioned him to leave the boy alone. It was clear that Aditya was deeply shaken and not in command of himself.

Mr Koya assembled the group around him. He pointed to the pressure gauge on his air cylinder signalling that everyone check theirs. The gauges indicated that the supply was limited. It was time to return.

Mr Koya led the way, holding Aditya by his hand. Vikram had no idea how Mr Koya located the boat. Everything looked the same underwater, no landmarks, just coral and sand stretching in all directions. Yet Mr Koya led them unerringly back to the anchor rope from where they spotted the hull of their boat floating above them.

They surfaced, removed their gear and started their return journey to Kadmat with Faisal at the wheel. On the deck, an agitated Captain Khan confronted his son.

'Stupid boy!' he exclaimed. 'I am going to thrash you right here, in front of everybody.' Grabbing Aditya's T-shirt, he jerked the boy towards him. 'Are you deaf or what? Mohammed warned all of us—particularly you— about the dangers of leaving the group, yet you disregarded him. Why is it that *you* always disobey instructions? Tell me why!' He raised his hand to strike Aditya.

Mr Koya was a foot shorter than both Aditya and his father. Yet he intervened, placing himself between them. He restrained Captain Khan. 'It's all right, Abbas, nothing happened. All's well that ends well.'

'No, all is not well,' fumed Captain Khan. 'This is not the first time this boy has disobeyed instructions. Ever since he was a child, he has disregarded authority.

This time, Aditya, you almost died. From the bottom of my heart, I pray that you have learnt a lesson, but knowing you, I wonder if you will ever learn.'

'Calm down, Abbas,' said Mr Koya. 'I will talk to the boy.' Turning, he gazed evenly at Aditya. 'Why did you leave the group?' he asked.

'I didn't leave on purpose,' mumbled Aditya. He stared at Mr Koya's feet, unable to look the instructor in the eye. 'I saw this turtle that was much bigger than the one you were following, and I set out after it. I had no intention of leaving the group . . . It just happened.'

'How come these things *happen* only to you?' barked Captain Khan. 'Why do they never happen to Vikram or Faisal?'

Mr Koya restrained his friend. 'Scuba diving might appear to be a simple sport, Aditya,' he said, 'but as you have personally experienced, it can turn life-threatening in seconds. That is why I spent so much time instructing you about safety and the rules of diving. Anything can happen underwater. You can run out of air, your air pipe can get tangled in rocks, a fish can attack, you can lose your way. That is why I always insist that we stay together in a group. The key to safety is being together. Even I never dive alone. When you left the group, Aditya, you broke the cardinal rule of scuba diving.'

Nobody said anything. The only sound was the drone of the motor and the crashing of the waves on the reef.

'Did the sharks scare you?' asked Vikram.

Aditya nodded, shuddering. 'I was frightened. There was nobody to help me. I was sure that they were going to attack.

My choice was either to turn away from them and be attacked or to meet them head-on . . . pretending I wasn't scared. I remembered what you had told us, Mr Koya, that reef sharks were harmless and don't usually attack.'

'And so you chose to go for them,' said Mr Koya. 'You are a brave boy, Aditya. Not many would have selected your course of action. I personally think that the sharks weren't heading for you. From where I was, it appeared that they were travelling towards another shark, behind you. When you changed direction and headed for them, they didn't know what to make of you. You must have unnerved them because they suddenly swam away from you. It was the force of their departure that sent you cartwheeling.' He looked appraisingly at Aditya. 'You are certainly a brave boy, but you are far too much an individualist. A person like you can endanger an entire group. I do not think I will ever allow you to dive with me again.'

Aditya looked down. There was nothing he could say. Mr Koya had every right to be disappointed in him.

Their entry into the lagoon was far smoother than their earlier exit. The colour of the water changed from dark blue to turquoise and finally brown as they motored across the sandy bed of the lagoon.

There was activity at the south end of the island. Boats were anchored there. A horde of uniformed people was swarming about the executive huts.

'Preparations for our guest have started,' said Mr Koya. 'You boys are lucky to be going away. When are you flying them out, Abbas?'

'We're scheduled to fly to Kalpeni on Friday,' replied Captain Khan. 'Three days from today. They'll have to wait it out.'

Vikram looked at the beach. It sparkled in the sun, stretching as far as he could see. He had grown fond of Kadmat. He would miss this lovely island.

KALPENI

Space is a precious commodity in the Lakshadweep Islands. Unlike the Andamans, which are geographically almost as large as the state of Goa, the islands of the Lakshadweep archipelago are small. So diminutive are they that it isn't possible to accommodate airstrips and runways on each of them. Just one island—Agatti—possesses an airport.

On the other hand, helipads are present on almost every island. No larger than a couple of basketball courts, helipads can be fitted anywhere. Helicopters are a lifeline for the people of Lakshadweep, particularly during the monsoons when the sea turns rough and boats can't ferry people between the islands.

The helicopter to Kalpeni Island took off on schedule on a Friday afternoon. A handful of passengers, most of them islanders, boarded the aircraft along with the boys. Captain Khan and his co-pilot, Mr Singh, were seated at the controls. An attendant settled the passengers in their seats. Then he fastened the doors, and after flashing a thumbs up signal to Captain Khan, he withdrew from the craft. The rotor blades started softly, spinning with a gentle whirring. This quickly intensified to a full-throated roar as they whipped away at high speed, creating a minor storm. Without warning, the ground fell away below them. When the helicopter had cleared the treetops, it paused and tilted its nose. Then with gut-wrenching speed, it climbed skyward in a sweeping curve. Vikram watched in fascination as the lagoon slipped by under. Soon the jagged wall of the coral reef appeared, half hidden by surging waves, and then the dark blue of the Arabian Sea.

The flight was uneventful to start with—the deep blue sea stretching as far as it was possible to see and the roar of helicopter blades numbing their ears. About halfway through the journey, Faisal suddenly pointed excitedly through the window.

'Whale, I've spotted a whale!' he yelled.

Vikram's heart leapt when he saw a shaft of white foam rising from the ink-blue water.

Captain Khan had seen the fountain of water too. An excited babble broke out in the aircraft as he banked the helicopter in a steep turn.

'There are two of them,' shouted Aditya.

'Three,' corrected Faisal. 'I see a third one too.'

Captain Khan spoke into his microphone. 'Blue whales,' he announced.

Vikram's mouth popped open. The whales were still far, but there was no doubting their immense size. They were long and rounded at the head, like submarines. Two were swimming side by side and a third one floated ahead.

The helicopter cut quickly across the water and soon the whales were beneath them. Their skin was dark—more grey, it seemed to Vikram, than blue. Water spouted from them, shooting skyward in fine white mists.

The significance of the moment overcame Vikram. He was looking down at the largest creatures on the planet. A lump formed in his throat. How magnificent they were, and how powerful. They were cutting through the water at a high speed, yet it was clear that they were barely using a fraction of their strength. Vikram couldn't help being reminded of a tiger he had once spotted in the forest of Ranthambore. It had been sauntering to a river, strength rippling from it with every step. The animal had exuded an aura of majesty. It was clear that it was the king of the forest. It was the same with the whales. They were the lords of the sea.

Captain Khan traced a circle around the whales. Their heads were broad and flat, and Vikram spotted their dorsal fin when they rose above the water. There were two more fins, up front, just behind their massive heads, and one more on their undulating tails.

The cabin buzzed with excitement and chatter. Only Vikram sat silently, his gaze riveted on the animals below. But he too joined in the chorus of 'oohs' when the whales, in unison, sank head first into the water. They paused for a moment, their tails hovering like mastheads above the water. Then with a casual flick of their flukes, they vanished beneath the waves.

The rest of the trip was uneventful and finally, the island of Kalpeni appeared as a speck on the horizon.

Balloon-like, it inflated in size till it occupied the horizon in front of them. Palm trees waved in the wind, the lagoon flashed by below and soon they were hovering over a tiny landing strip.

Shortly after touching down, Captain Khan stepped out to bid goodbye to the boys.

'I see that big grin on your face, Aditya,' said Captain Khan, looking at his son. 'Like Rusty again before his morning walk.'

Aditya stuck his hands out as if they were paws. 'Pant, pant, pant,' he huffed, tongue hanging from his mouth.

Everyone laughed.

'Of course I'm like Rusty, Dad. An entire week on this island. What would you expect? It's going to be awesome.'

Captain Khan looked gravely at his son. 'Don't do anything stupid, Aditya. There's no Uncle Koya to get you out of trouble here.'

'Vikram's here, Dad. The responsible one. Isn't that what you call him? He'll look after me.'

Vikram laughed. 'We'll be fine, Uncle Abbas, don't worry.'

Captain Khan winked. 'I'm sure you will.'

There was a call from the helicopter. Mr Singh, the co-pilot, was waving.

Captain Khan hugged each of the boys. 'Have fun. I'll be back to pick you up in a week. And Faisal, do convey my greetings to your uncle, Basheer.'

The helicopter departed in a storm of dust. Silence fell upon the island as the machine shrank to a speck and then disappeared altogether.

Basheer Koya's home wasn't far. A few minutes' walk, said Faisal. He led them to a concrete road that weaved through a forest of palm trees. They walked past several modest single-storeyed homes set back among the trees. Vikram noticed that here too, as in Kadmat, the doors to most of the homes were open. Faisal had explained that there were hardly any cases of robberies in the islands. So islanders didn't bother to lock their doors.

Aditya nudged Vikram, pointing at Faisal.

Their friend was walking with his head down.

'The uncle,' whispered Vikram.

'Yes.' Aditya nodded. 'Doesn't look very keen to be meeting him, does he?'

Faisal's face darkened when they halted before a large double-storeyed house by the sea.

'Is this the place?' whispered Vikram.

'Must be,' replied Aditya in a soft tone. He made a face as he looked at it. 'It's kind of different, isn't it?'

'It sure is,' said Vikram.

Basheer Koya's home stood out from the rest. *But not in a nice manner*, thought Vikram. In stark contrast with the earth-coloured Kalpeni homes, this house was painted a startling purple with red columns that flashed brightly in the afternoon sun. Barriers and fences were mostly absent on the island, but Basheer Koya's home was sealed behind a high concrete wall. Palm trees were conspicuously absent; there was not a single one in his compound. The house looked like it didn't belong. It was as if someone had parked a gaudy cruise ship on the island.

An imposing wrought-iron gate barred their way. Faisal pushed it aside and entered. Inside, an old man with a bent back was mopping the porch.

'Hullo, Ismail,' greeted Faisal.

The man looked up. His face was wrinkled and his back hunched. Oddly, in spite of his age, he had a full head of jet-black hair, neatly combed and swept back behind his ears. Ismail did not smile at Faisal, nor did he acknowledge his greeting. He propped his mop against the wall and walked to a large wooden door, which he pushed open. The boys followed.

The hall was dark. Curtains were drawn across the windows, allowing only the faintest of glows inside. In the dim light, Vikram saw several carvings and statues. There was a flight of stairs to one side. Ismail steered them up the stairs to a door on the upper floor, which he opened and ushered them inside.

This room was dark too, although less than the hall. Aditya strode to the windows and pushed the curtains aside.

Ismail turned to Faisal and addressed him squeakily in the local island language, which neither Vikram nor Aditya could understand.

Aditya hissed loudly. 'Come here, Vikram,' he said excitedly.

Vikram crossed to where his friend stood and inhaled sharply. 'Wow!' he whispered.

Outside, a turquoise sea twinkled beneath a bright blue sky, and a palm-fringed beach stretched as far as the eye could see.

Aditya stared in glee at Vikram. The boys exchanged a high five.

Faisal joined them at the window. 'Give me a five too,' he said, raising his hand.

The three friends leapt and clapped their hands together. 'Hey,' said Aditya. 'Look at Faisal, Vikram. He's grinning like a monkey.' He turned to the islander. 'What's up?' he asked. 'Won a lottery or something?'

Faisal punched the air with his hands. 'My uncle!' he exclaimed. 'He isn't here on Kalpeni. I don't have to meet him today.'

'Yay!' shouted Vikram. 'Great for you, Faisal. No worries then.'

'What are we waiting for?' cried Aditya. 'Let's hit the beach!'

'This way,' said Faisal. There was another door to the room. It opened out to a small landing and from there a set of stairs led straight down, bypassing the hall. Faisal led the way and pushing aside a metal gate, they ran on to the beach.

The sand was hot. The boys raced to the water's edge where it was cool and wet and firm.

Shielding his eyes from the sun, Vikram looked out across the Kalpeni lagoon. Like Kadmat, Kalpeni was an atoll, ringed on all sides by a coral reef. Faisal had said that the lagoon here was one of the largest in the Lakshadweep archipelago. There are several islands within the lagoon of which Kalpeni was the biggest. The rest were too small for habitation.

'The jetty,' said Faisal, pointing to where a long concrete platform jutted out into the water. 'That's where we need to go. We'll find Shaukat there.'

Shaukat was Faisal's friend. His father ran the water sports centre on Kalpeni. It was Shaukat's father who had worked under Mr Koya at Kadmat before being promoted as the chief of the new Kalpeni Water Sports Centre.

Dragging his leg in the sand, Aditya traced a large ring, encircling Vikram and Faisal. 'What's with this dude Ismail?' he asked. 'He doesn't strike me as a great fan of yours, Faisal.'

'You noticed, did you?'

'Come on,' said Aditya. 'We would have to be blind to not see that.'

The bleak look returned to Faisal's face. 'Why do you think I didn't want to come here? There isn't anybody who likes me in this house. With Ismail, it's even worse. It goes a long way back. I've played pranks on him and he's never liked them. Like mixing colours into his hair dye.' Faisal paused, his eyes lighting up. 'You should have seen his face when his hair turned blue.'

'So I take it he isn't your best friend.' Vikram laughed.

'No, he isn't. And neither is my Uncle Basheer.' Faisal's face darkened again. 'I just have this one day without him. Ismail says Uncle Basheer is returning tomorrow morning.'

'So forget about him for today,' said Aditya. 'Come on. Last one to the jetty buys ice cream for all.'

The boys sprinted to the jetty.

The jetty was broad enough for a car to drive on and it stretched far into the lagoon. Several fishing boats floated alongside, moored to the pillars that supported it. They found Shaukat halfway down the jetty, squatting on the railing, working on a fishing net.

Like most islanders, Shaukat was short and dark. He sported a small moustache and his hair was neatly combed back over his forehead. A smile sprang to his face when he spotted them.

Dropping his net, he ran to Faisal and embraced him. They broke into an animated conversation conducted entirely in their language.

When they were done, Faisal introduced Shaukat.

'Welcome to Kalpeni.' He smiled, flashing his bright teeth. 'We've been expecting you.'

'Dad called and talked with Shaukat's father,' explained Faisal.

'Yes,' said Shaukat. 'He spoke about a fishing trip and also about visiting nearby islands.'

Vikram and Aditya looked at each other.

'That would be great,' said Aditya.

'Have you arranged a boat?' asked Faisal.

'It's done,' said Shaukat. 'Come along, I'll show it to you. It's at the far end of the jetty.'

A warm feeling spread inside Vikram. This was working out just right. Kalpeni could turn out to be as much fun as Kadmat, if not more.

There wasn't much activity on the jetty. The boats tied alongside were mostly empty. Vikram spotted seagulls as he followed Shaukat and his friends. They perched on the railing, watching idly as the boys walked past.

'Here we are,' said Shaukat when they came to a wall where the jetty ended. He pointed at the water, at the very last boat. 'This is the *Alisha*.'

The *Alisha* was a typical island boat, with its engine at the centre and a navigation platform at the rear. It was identical to Mr Koya's diving boat, except that its sunroof was longer, covering the entire deck area.

They descended the stairs and entered the boat.

'There's room to store supplies for a week or more,' observed Vikram, looking at the hold.

'Supplies won't be a problem,' said Shaukat. 'But first we have to decide where we are going.'

'You tell us,' said Faisal. 'I remember Dad speaking about some sandbanks not far from here.'

'Yes, there are sandbanks nearby,' said Shaukat. 'To the north. About three hours by boat. That's one of our options. The other is the Tinakara-Pitti Islands. They lie to the south. Both have good coral and are great for snorkelling.' Shaukat paused a moment, thinking. 'If I had to choose, I would go to the islands. Mainly because they are big with lots of space. The sandbanks are small—just strips of sand that stick out from the sea. But there's a hitch with the islands. They are far. About ten to twelve hours by boat.'

'That is far,' said Faisal. 'Twenty-four hours, just travelling to and fro.' He shook his head. 'The sandbanks make more sense to me.'

'That's what I've been thinking too,' said Shaukat.

'You're the captain, Shaukat,' said Aditya. 'We'll go with whatever you say. Right, Vikram?'

Vikram nodded. 'If it's the sandbanks, that's where we will go.'

So it was settled. Shaukat said that he would stock the boat the next day and they would leave the day after. The boys chatted through the afternoon discussing the various supplies to be carried for the trip and the fishing gear.

Later, in the evening, Shaukat offered the boys a reef walk. The tide was low, he said. The only time it was possible to walk on the reef.

Shaukat chose a small boat for their excursion. They cast off from the Kalpeni shore and rowed out into the lagoon. At first, the water was deep and the reef far in the distance. After a while, they came to what looked like a scattering of boulders and the water turned shallow. It was knee-deep when they stepped out and Shaukat anchored the boat. Faisal led the way, wading towards the dark rocklike boulders.

The water they treaded was alive with marine creatures. Sea cucumbers rested placidly in the sand and there were shells of all shapes and colours. Tiny fish and crabs darted here and there.

'Those aren't rocks,' said Shaukat, pointing ahead. 'That's coral you are looking at. That's the reef—the very highest point of the reef. Low tide is the only time you can view it. The rest of the time, the sea submerges it.'

Soon they were walking on the reef. It was hard and slippery and there were pools of water everywhere.

'It's so colourless,' said Vikram. 'Nothing like the coral we saw when we dived.'

Aditya nodded. 'It looks dead to me,' he said.

'The coral here is mostly dead,' said Shaukat. 'It's been dead for a long time. What you are walking on is its skeleton.' He pointed to blue waters of the sea. 'Out there in the sea, when you go under the water—that's where the living coral is. That's where you find the beauty, the colour and the fish too.'

Faisal had halted. He was peering at a pool of water. There were several colourful shell-like creatures with thick bulbous lips there.

'Clams,' said Shaukat, pointing at one of the mouth-like shells.

'Wow!' said Vikram. 'Look at their colours.'

'Way out,' said Aditya, bending forward.

'They are beautiful,' said Shaukat. 'They wait for the current to carry food to them. The moment anything enters their mouth, they clamp their lips shut and eat it up.'

'Watch,' said Faisal. He plucked a blade of seagrass and inserted it between the lips of the clam. For a moment, nothing happened. Then the lips started to move, clamping on the blade of grass. Suddenly a jet of water shot out from the clam, catching Aditya, who was watching closely, on his face. With a startled yell, he fell over backwards into the water. Vikram looked on in concern, but both the islanders were laughing.

They continued their walk, Aditya more warily now.

To one side, there was a group of fishermen. They were standing thigh-deep in the water, peering at the coral. They were fishing for octopus, explained Shaukat. The slippery eight-legged creatures liked to hide in the cracks and crevices of the reef.

Eventually, they came to a place where they could go no further. The coral was wet and slippery and covered with clumps of green algae. Ahead lay the open sea, its waves striking the coral with a force that generated a salty spray. The reef was hard, unyielding and sharp. No wonder so many boats had met their end on it. Vikram shuddered at the thought of being trapped there in a storm. There would be no hope of survival.

An uneasiness crept into Vikram as he stood there. It was as if he was trespassing a forbidden zone. This section of the reef was an eerie place. Only during the brief moments of the lowest tide did the sea reluctantly relinquish it, before submerging it once again under racing waves. This was not a place for humans. It belonged to the sea and all its myriad creatures who lived and died within its life-sustaining embrace.

Far in the distance, the sun was setting on the western horizon. Tomorrow, they would buy provisions and stock the boat while Faisal would spend time with his uncle. The day after, they would sail across the sea to the sandbanks. Such was their plan, but little did they dream of what the future had in store for them.

WINDSURFING THE LAGOON

Vikram woke up at the crack of dawn. While Faisal and Aditya slept, he slipped out of the gate and on to the beach.

It was another one of those beautiful island mornings. The sun was orange and gold and the sky was bright, smudged here and there with wisps of cloud.

Something niggled at Vikram. An odd feeling. He wondered what it could be. Then he saw the lagoon. On most days, its waters were smooth with not a wrinkle on them. A gentle rippling was the most turbulent it ever got. But today it was transformed. Waves curled everywhere on its surface. The entire bay was heaving. It was as if a monster octopus had submerged itself in the lagoon and was twitching and flailing its arms underwater.

Then Vikram noticed the wind. It was blowing so hard that the trunks of the palm trees were bent backwards. For a moment, Vikram experienced a sinking feeling. Could there be a storm brewing? That would be a shame because bad weather would scuttle their excursion plans.

But his worry faded as quickly as it came. Out at the edge of the lagoon, fishing boats were chugging out to sea. They wouldn't be venturing out of the lagoon if a storm was on its way.

Vikram stretched. The weather was perfect for a run.

Starting forward, he splashed into the water, running to where it was knee-deep. He weaved out to where the sand was dry and then back into the water. He dodged waves when they surged across the sand. Tiny sandpiper birds skittered out of his way. Gulls flapped their wings and flew away. Crabs scooted across the sand, burrowing deep when he drew near.

Vikram ran with his hands outstretched, enjoying himself. The wind refreshed and invigorated him. Except for a few fishermen prodding at their nets, the beach was empty. He passed the jetty and kept running. Further down there were huts along the beach. One of them had a banner with 'Kalpeni Water Sports Centre' written on it. Vikram pulled up when he saw someone sitting on the sand outside it.

Shaukat.

Shaukat had seen him and was waving. Vikram ran forward and halted by his side.

'Super morning for running,' panted Vikram, clutching his hips.

Shaukat smiled. There was a screwdriver in his hand. Lying at his feet was a dismembered windsurf mast.

'Nice morning for windsurfing too,' he said.

'Yes, the wind is blowing, isn't it?'

'Want to sail?' offered the islander.

Vikram looked out at the lagoon. 'Those waves. What do you call them? Sailors have a name for them, don't they?'

'We call them white caps, some say white horses.'

'White' was an apt description, thought Vikram. The water was furrowed with pale, frothing streaks.

'White caps are a sign that there is a strong wind blowing. The conditions are perfect for windsurfing. Why don't you take a board out?'

Vikram looked uncertainly at Shaukat. 'Alone?' he asked.

The islander's eyes twinkled. 'That's the only way to learn. Faisal told me that you know the basics well.'

'I can sail,' said Vikram. 'But only in light winds. Not in conditions like these.'

Shaukat waved dismissively. 'No need to worry. I'll keep a lookout. Take this as a challenge. It will be hard. But if you get going—and I'm sure you will—you'll enjoy yourself. Come on, I'll rig a board for you.'

Brushing sand off his legs, Shaukat rose and entered the hut. There were several windsurf boards and sails stacked on shelves in a corner. Selecting a board and a short sail, he carried them to the water.

Vikram removed his T-shirt and hung it on a peg in the hut. Then he ran down to where Shaukat waited by the shore.

Vikram looked on as the islander attached the sail to the board. His quiet skilfulness inspired confidence. It was only because of Shaukat's assurance that Vikram was attempting a sail. The conditions in the lagoon were distinctly stormy.

'Here,' said Shaukat, handing Vikram the board. 'Stay away from the reef and don't go too far. Enjoy your sail. We can have breakfast at my place afterwards.'

Vikram stepped into the water, pulling the board behind him. There was a nervous flutter in his stomach. The board rocked and swayed in the water. Vikram held it steady and stepped on to it. He stood lightly, countering the choppiness of the water. Then leaning back, he pulled at the sail. Water drained from it. When it emerged, the wind shook it violently. It bucked and strained in Vikram's hand.

'Steady,' shouted Shaukat from the shore.

The board was turning unstable under Vikram's feet. If he didn't get it moving soon, he would fall into the water. He yanked the sail towards him and in a quick motion transferred his hands to the boom, which encircled the sail at shoulder level. The board responded instantly. It jerked, almost toppling Vikram. Then it shot forward as the wind powered the sail. Vikram hung on tight as the board quickly gained speed.

'You did it!' yelled Shaukat. 'Way to go!'

Vikram grinned.

The bow of the windsurf cut through the water like a knife, working up a spray, which drenched the lower half of his body. The sail shook and shuddered. It tugged at Vikram, threatening to pull him over. He shifted his weight, leaning backwards. The board accelerated, clipping the waves. He was moving so fast that his eyes were starting to water. Unbidden, a roar burst forth from deep inside Vikram. Nothing, absolutely nothing, could top this heady feeling of power and speed. He felt as one with the wind and the water.

Vikram zipped up and down the lagoon. He startled shoals of fish that arced across his path and disappeared. The wind howled. It pulled at the sail, striving to tear it from his hands. Vikram fought hard. He hung on grimly. His wrists ached and at times, his shoulders felt like they might pop from their sockets. It was a silent hard-fought battle with no clear victor. Often the wind would contemptuously fling him face down into the water. But for brief electrifying moments, Vikram would tame the wind, trapping it in his sail and propelling his board at a breathtaking speed.

After an hour of high-spirited joy, Vikram saw a board with a yellow sail leave the shore. Travelling at high speed, it made its way towards him.

Aditya.

Vikram dropped his sail and jumped into the water, which surprisingly was barely neck-deep.

Aditya arrived in a spectacular flurry of water, braking from full speed to a dead halt.

He was in high spirits. 'Wow,' he shouted. 'What a wind!'

Vikram raised his hand and the friends high-fived.

'It's so shallow here,' said Aditya, leaping into the water too.

'Odd, isn't it?' Vikram glanced at the shore. 'We are about a kilometre out and yet we can stand. Strange places, these lagoons.'

'Who cares,' said Aditya. 'All I know is that they are super for windsurfing.' He smacked Vikram on his shoulder. 'That was great stuff, bro. Top-class windsurfing. No one will say you are a beginner any more.'

Vikram grinned. 'Want to race?' he asked.

Aditya stared. 'You? You think you can race me?'

'Why not?' said Vikram. 'You saw me just now. I was flying on the water.'

'*Flying*?' exclaimed Aditya. 'You call that flying. Hah!' He threw his head back and laughed. 'I'll show you.'

'Show me,' retorted Vikram, reaching for his board.

Aditya leapt on to his board and grabbed his sail.

They set off, racing up and down the lagoon. Aditya was far better than Vikram. There was simply no comparison. It was as if the wind was his friend. He could coax more power from it than all, save the champions of the sport. Aditya was in a mood to show off. He celebrated his mastery over the wind with a spectacular display of control. Vikram could only watch as Aditya wove circles around him.

They were tired but happy when they turned back to the shore.

'Hey, is that Shaukat there?' asked Aditya as they sailed past the jetty.

Lowering his sail, Vikram spotted the islander on board the *Alisha*, waving at them.

The boys changed direction, heading for the boat.

'Had fun?' asked Shaukat, helping them haul their boards into the boat.

'The best time of my life,' exulted Vikram.

Aditya made a sniggering sound. 'He thought he could beat me. But he learnt otherwise soon enough.'

'He did a fine job,' said Shaukat. 'For a beginner, that was great windsurfing, Vikram. Well done.'

'Top-class,' admitted Aditya. He patted Vikram on his back. 'My friend is a quick learner.'

The boys helped Shaukat de-rig the boards. The sails were washed and carefully wrapped around the masts. The equipment was packed in a tarpaulin and stowed away.

'How come you are here?' asked Vikram when they were done.

'Boat inspection,' said Shaukat. 'We have a long journey tomorrow. I worry and keep checking things.' He smiled. 'That's me, I can't help it.' He pointed to the fore section of the boat where towels and clothes were heaped. 'I've brought your things here. You can dry yourselves and get ready.'

'Where's Faisal?' asked Shaukat as the boys towelled themselves.

'He won't be joining us today,' said Aditya. 'His uncle is arriving at 10 a.m.' He looked at his watch. 'He should have arrived by now.'

'Uh-huh,' said Shaukat, shaking his head. He pointed out to the sea where a ship was visible. 'That's the *Tipu Sultan*, the ferry that operates between the islands and the mainland. His uncle will be on that boat. It's still half an hour away.'

'What a bonehead Faisal is,' said Aditya. 'He could easily have enjoyed the morning with us. But he refused. He was in a terrible mood.'

Shaukat laughed. 'He's always in a bad mood when his uncle is around. That's no secret. Everyone on the island knows that.'

Aditya grinned crookedly. 'Well, his mood got even worse when I told him we'd be spending the day with you, and not with him and his uncle.'

'Oh,' said Vikram. 'I didn't know that. Wasn't the plan to meet his uncle?'

'Yes. We'll be meeting him. But in the evening instead. I couldn't let such a beautiful day go to waste. Faisal, of course, didn't like that. He called us traitors. Colourful language followed.' Aditya laughed, remembering.

'Typical,' said Shaukat, smiling. 'I'm glad you did though. There's lots for us to do today. There's supplies to be bought, equipment to be checked. But first, let's head home for breakfast.'

'Now that's what I call a great idea,' said Aditya.

'I second that,' said Vikram.

Shaukat grinned. 'Let's go,' he said. 'My home is nearby. Just five minutes from here.'

BASHEER KOYA

Faisal *was* in a bad mood. His uncle's impending arrival hovered like a dark cloud over him. And his friends' decision to abandon him for the day only made things worse.

Faisal had noticed the wind the moment he had strolled out on to the beach, and his mood had soured even further when he saw his friends enjoying themselves. He wished he had accepted Aditya's offer as he watched them speed their boards across the lagoon. But it was too late now. His uncle would be arriving shortly.

Faisal sat under a palm tree. He passed time by drawing figures in the sand. Above him, palm fronds shook and fluttered as the wind whistled through them. The sun shone brightly. The sand intensified its glare, forcing Faisal to shut his eyes. It was pleasant under the tree and the wind was crisp and enjoyable. The rustling of the palms overhead soothed him and he soon fell asleep.

The tide slowly crept up the beach and finally washed over Faisal's feet, waking him with a start. He looked at his watch, muttering softly to himself. It was past midday.

Basheer uncle would have arrived by now. He dusted sand from his clothes and rose hurriedly to his feet.

Faisal heard raised voices from the living room window when he entered the yard. He crept forward till he was below the window and peeped in.

His uncle was standing in the centre of the room, facing a group of men.

Basheer Koya was a copy of Faisal's father, except that he was fatter and there was hardly any hair on his head. But unlike his brother, whose manner was calm and collected, Basheer Koya's face was contorted with rage. His cheeks were dark and red and he was shouting like a man possessed.

'Fools!' thundered Basheer Koya in Malayalam. 'Monkeys have more brains than you lot. Idiots. I thought you had ears. But obviously you don't. You weren't to set foot in Kalpeni. How many times did I tell you not to come here? Yet, not only do you come to the island, but even more brainlessly, you visit my home.'

A bearded man with big, wide shoulders spoke. 'Sir,' he began. 'Sir—'

Basheer Koya ranted on, cutting off the man. 'I travelled all the way to Kochi to make certain that no suspicion fell on me and I returned only after the operation was over. And you? I come home and see you fools sitting in my house. I take all these precautions and now everyone on this island can link me to you and from there to the operation.'

'But, sir—'

'You were under orders to head to Tinakara Island. What are you doing here?'

'Sir. I was trying to explain just that, sir. We were headed for Tinakara. But we had engine trouble, sir. A terrible rattling noise came from the engine and we were forced to head for the nearest island. You can speak to the mechanic, sir. He looked at our boat and said we were lucky to make it here to Kalpeni.'

The explanation diminished Basheer Koya's rage, yet he continued to glare at the bearded man. 'Kumar. Where is Kumar?' he barked.

'Kumar is safely on board, sir. There's no need to worry about him. He is in the lower cabin and one of our men is with him all the time. He can't make a sound or do anything. He won't be able to alert the mechanics.'

Faisal froze. This was not for his ears. It was wrong of him to eavesdrop. He wondered if he should leave, but who was Kumar and what was his uncle up to?

'No one is to know that we have a prisoner on board,' growled Basheer Koya. 'Even Allah will not be able to help you if he is discovered. I make no allowances for mistakes.' Basheer Koya stared at his men, shifting his gaze from one to the other. 'Do you understand?'

There was silence in the room.

Faisal understood full well what his uncle meant. He shuddered. These were horrible threats, and it was his uncle who was mouthing them.

'Do you understand?' repeated Basheer Koya.

The men nodded, dropping their heads.

Basheer Koya scowled and turned away.

At the window, Faisal quickly ducked.

A sofa protested as Basheer Koya settled himself on it. His voice was more composed when he spoke next. 'I have heard that the operation went off smoothly. Give me the details, Krishnan.'

The tension eased in the room. The relief was so palpable that Faisal sensed it too. Rising, he looked in again.

'Everything went as per your plan, sir,' said Krishnan, the bearded man who had spoken earlier, his voice noticeably perkier now. 'We set off from Kavaratti Island. Our departure was uneventful, like we hoped it would be. We told everybody that we were on a fishing trip. We did spend the first day fishing, but the next day we set sail for Kadmat.

'You were right about the heightened security at Kadmat, sir. Two naval vessels intercepted us as we entered the Kadmat lagoon. They escorted us to the jetty and boarded our boat. They wanted to know what we were doing at Kadmat. We told them that we were from Kavaratti Island and that we were out on a fishing trip. Our engine was giving us trouble and we had come to Kadmat to have it fixed. We showed them our papers and they were satisfied. They went away after warning us not to venture towards the south end of the island.'

'Later, in the afternoon, I walked down the beach to have a look at the security arrangements. The southern end of the island was cordoned off. They had laid barbed wire across the beach and there were guards with machine guns. Three powerboats patrolled the shore. The security was impressive. You couldn't approach the island from the beach or the sea.

'Kumar was being put up at the presidential huts, at the southern tip of the island. The only access point to the huts was a road, which was barricaded and guarded 24/7. There was a helipad near the barricades and I made my way there. The guards didn't seem to care about my presence and I stood there looking at the huts. '

'Did you see Mammen and Abdul?' asked Basheer Koya.

'I didn't get to see Abdul, sir. But I spotted Mammen. He was walking up and down the place, flitting in and out of rooms. He had been assigned the task of looking after Kumar.'

'I know that,' said Basheer Koya, 'I arranged the job for him.'

'Selecting Mammen was a master stroke, sir. Even Abdul and Muthu.'

The glimmering of a smile appeared on Basheer Koya's face. 'Yes,' he said. 'All three of them were indispensable. This became clear to me when I started planning.' The sofa squeaked as Basheer Koya leaned back. 'Go on,' he said. 'What happened next?'

Faisal felt a chill of comprehension creep through him. The unthinkable had happened. It was all beginning to make sense. Kumar was the Tamilian from Sri Lanka who had been brought to Lakshadweep for his protection. It was because of Kumar that Kadmat had been turned into a fortress and they had been forced to leave. Now it appeared that his uncle had masterminded a plot to kidnap Kumar.

Krishnan continued: 'As per the plan, I approached the guards at the presidential huts. I told them that Mammen was my cousin and that I wished to meet him. Mammen came out and we put on a show for the guards, acting like relatives who hadn't seen each other in years. Our performance was convincing because the guards lost interest and left us alone.

'When we were out of earshot, Mammen told me everything was going to plan. He had established a routine of serving coffee to the guards and to Kumar each night after dinner. That night he planned to blend a sleeping concoction into their coffee. He asked me to return at 1 a.m. He assured me that the guards and Kumar would be knocked out by then.'

'And how about Abdul? Did he carry out his tasks as instructed?' asked Basheer Koya.

'Yes, sir. Abdul is a first-rate electrician. He ensured that the fluorescent lights around the bunker and the helipad failed after midnight. Everything was dark when I arrived and the guards were fast asleep. I walked to Kumar's room without any trouble. Inside, the man was completely knocked out. Mammen told me he had stirred in a double dose of his concoction into Kumar's coffee. We had no trouble carrying him away on our shoulders. We slipped past the security guards, crossed the helipad and reached the road where our people were waiting to transport him to the boat.'

Basheer Koya clapped his hands in glee. 'And what about Muthu?' he asked. 'My inspirational choice! How did that play out?'

Krishnan laughed. 'You were right, sir. Muthu is a photocopy of Kumar. Their skin colour is the same. Their height is the same. They are like twins, sir. Even their mothers will not be able to identify which one is their son!'

Basheer Koya rocked on the sofa, laughing and clapping.

'Sir, switching Kumar for Muthu turned out to be the easiest part of the operation. Muthu returned with Mammen to the huts after Kumar was taken away. Before leaving he told me that not only was he looking forward to a nice holiday, but even more so to having Mammen as his assistant. He joked, saying he was going to give Mammen a rough time, ordering him about and making him work hard.'

Basheer Koya clapped again. He gave Krishnan a long, appraising look. 'You have done well, Krishnan,' he said.

Krishnan beamed with pleasure.

Basheer Koya rubbed his palms together. 'All is going according to plan. Muthu is clearly doing a great job of impersonating Kumar. No one is aware that the real Kumar has been kidnapped! But it isn't safe having Kumar here on Kalpeni. He should be out at sea, or on Tinakara Island.'

'Sir,' said Krishnan. 'It is finalized then that we are handing Kumar over to the militants at Tinakara. Last time we spoke, you had said that you were still to confirm.'

Basheer Koya nodded. 'Yes. I have confirmed with them. It is fixed. When will your boat be ready for departure?'

'Tonight, sir.'

'Good. Then leave for Tinakara first thing in the morning.'

'Sir,' said Krishnan. 'There's one thing we need to consult on. It's the wind, sir. It's stronger than forecasted. There could be a storm on the way.'

Basheer Koya rubbed his stomach. He had thought that with Kumar's successful abduction, the perilous segment of the operation was behind him. But the impending storm complicated matters. Serious thought had to be given to it. He called Krishnan over. They needed to discuss this unanticipated hazard.

Faisal stood below the window, struggling to process what he had heard. His uncle . . . his father's younger brother . . . He had stooped to kidnapping. Faisal was numbed. His head was spinning. He steadied himself, leaning against the wall.

There was a rustling sound nearby. Someone was standing behind him. But Faisal did not register the intruder's presence. His mind was in a daze. A cold hand snaked across his body and pushed him hard against the wall.

FAISAL

Vikram and Aditya spent the entire day with Shaukat. Vikram experienced the occasional twinge of guilt for abandoning Faisal, but Aditya had no qualms at all. 'Look,' said Aditya, when Vikram expressed his discomfort. 'His uncle is a nasty man. Faisal has repeatedly told us so. Why would you want to waste your time with him? Feel the wind, Vikram. It's a lovely day. Who would you like to spend it with—Shaukat or Basheer Koya? It's a no-brainer.' Vikram could not dispute Aditya. It was a wonderful day indeed. And Shaukat was infinitely better company than Basheer Koya.

The boys accompanied Shaukat to the market to purchase provisions for their excursion. The islander insisted on buying canned food. Canned food was waterproof, he explained. It wouldn't get spoiled. They carried the provisions to the *Alisha* and stocked her hold. Then they collected two large jerrycans from the water sports institute and filled them with drinking water. Lugging the cans to the boat was hard work. They all pitched in.

Later, they had lunch at Shaukat's home. His mother served a meal of fish curry and rice and the boys expressed their appreciation, licking their plates and fingers clean. They lazed in the veranda afterwards, sitting and chatting. Vikram tired soon. He had woken early and the morning windsurfing had been hard work. He blinked and yawned, and Shaukat suggested that they rest for a while. The boys spread themselves on the veranda and soon fell asleep. It was late by the time they woke and they soon had to leave for Basheer Koya's place.

Shaukat cautioned them about the weather before they left. 'There shouldn't be a problem,' he said, 'but you can never tell. I'll finish the packing tonight in any case and, weather permitting, we will leave at 8 a.m. tomorrow.'

Vikram and Aditya ambled along the road. The setting sun had painted the sky orange. Street lights flickered on. Islanders strolled alongside, laughing and chatting with one another. Cyclists pedalled past, ringing their bells.

'Basheer Koya is home,' said Aditya as they neared the house. 'Look at the lights. They're all turned on.'

'The good times are over, I guess,' said Vikram. 'Can't duck the man any more.'

Entering the walled compound, the boys rang the doorbell. Ismail opened the door. Vikram wondered at the curious smirk on his face as he let them in.

The living room was crowded with men. Cigarette vapour hung like mist in the air. The lights were turned low and it was hard to see. The men were mostly bearded and many wore lungis. A heavyset man with bulging cheeks sat smoking on a rocking chair to one side. His features were so similar to Faisal's dad that it was easy to tell that he was Basheer Koya.

Basheer Koya smiled. 'So you are Faisal's friends. I am his uncle.'

'Pleased to meet you, sir,' said Aditya.

'You have a wonderful home, Mr Koya,' said Vikram. 'Thank you for allowing us to stay here.'

Basheer Koya waved expansively. 'You are welcome, boys. Stay as long as you like. But I have bad news for you. Your friend had to leave for Kadmat suddenly. One of our relatives has fallen ill. I would have travelled with him, but I have just arrived from the mainland and there are pressing matters that need my attention here.'

Vikram and Aditya stared dumbfounded at each other.

'He left without telling us?' asked a bewildered Aditya.

Basheer Koya flicked ash from his cigarette. 'Yes. That's how it was. The decision to travel was taken on the spot. We received the call in the afternoon and a ferryboat was scheduled to travel to Kadmat just minutes later. There was no time to even pack his clothes. My poor nephew, he was terribly upset. He requested that I explain his sudden departure to you. He did not want to ruin your holiday. He asked if you boys could stay on.' Basheer Koya sighed. 'You are Faisal's friends. Of course, you are welcome to stay on.'

Vikram looked at the ground in a daze. Aditya's mouth had popped open.

'It is natural that you boys are upset. I would be too if my friend had to leave so abruptly. But there's no need to worry, you can still have a good time here. Ismail says you

71

are friends with Shaukat. He is a good boy and will keep you entertained.' Basheer Koya's lips twitched, shaping a smile that barely creased his cheeks. 'You are tired. It's been a long day on the beach. Go and wash up. Ismail will serve you an early dinner upstairs if you wish.'

Neither of the boys had any intention of eating dinner with Basheer Koya and his cronies.

'Thank you, sir,' said Vikram. 'We are tired and would like to eat upstairs.'

'Please.' Basheer Koya beamed. 'You are most welcome. I will see you tomorrow morning. We can get to know each other then.' He smiled again, and as if dismissing them, he turned his attention to his guests.

Basheer Koya waited till the boys had shut their doors behind them. He then turned to Krishnan. 'Come with me,' he said. 'I'm going for a walk. I want you to join me.'

Krishnan looked at his boss. A walk? Now? When he was enjoying his drink? But it was Basheer Koya who had requested him. Sighing, he rose and followed Basheer Koya to the door. Outside, Basheer Koya led Krishnan to the beach through the back gate. They walked for a while, enjoying the wind blowing in from the sea.

Basheer Koya kicked at a crab that was scuttling across the sand. 'This is about my nephew, Faisal, and his friends,' he said. 'We have a problem.'

'It is a problem, sir,' acknowledged Krishnan. 'Faisal knows everything. What do you plan to do with him?'

'If he wasn't my nephew, I would have dealt with him already. But he is my brother's son.' Basheer Koya gestured with his hands. 'The problem right now are his friends. It is clear that they don't believe my story about Faisal abandoning them.' Basheer Koya snorted. 'I didn't expect them to. It is a stupid story. I am certain that they will call my brother tomorrow and inquire about Faisal. That's when everything I've said will come apart.'

'True, sir,' said Krishnan. 'We can't let that happen.'

'Exactly. We can't let that happen. So here's what we'll do. Ismail will serve the boys their dinner while we continue our party. I see no need to abandon it. Later, when we are done, we will overpower and tie them up. Then we will transfer all three of them to my boat.' Basheer Koya paused, a troubled expression darkening his pudgy features. 'Talking about boats, this wind is bothering me. What does the latest forecast say?'

'No rains predicted, sir. But there is bad weather to the south of us. Chances are that it won't affect us if we leave for Tinakara tomorrow.'

'Good,' breathed Basheer Koya. 'That's one worry off my head. There is a change of plan, however. I'll be coming with you and so will my nephew and the boys. We have no choice but to evacuate the boys before questions are asked. I had work to do here, but it will have to wait. Who knows, maybe it's the right thing to do. I should be with you and Kumar at this stage, not sitting here on Kalpeni. Load the boys into my private boat, and fuel and stock it tomorrow. I will decide what to do with the boys once we've handed Kumar over and collected the money.'

Krishnan smiled at his boss. 'I'm glad to have you along, sir. I was nervous about the militants. You know them well and have dealt with them.'

Basheer Koya remained silent. Indeed, he knew the militants well. He was one of their largest arm suppliers and had been dealing with them for years. They trusted him and that was why they had sought his help for Kumar's kidnapping. He had already passed on the news of the success of the mission and they had conveyed their jubilation and delight.

There was a lightness in Basheer Koya's step as he turned and walked back to his house. The challenge had been almost insurmountable, but he had pulled it off. This was a huge achievement, one of the many feathers in his cap, and certainly the finest. The militants had already congratulated him. Their respect and regard for him was sky-high. Not only was he set to make a lot of money, but from now on, he wouldn't have to worry about work any more. He had proved his value. Work would flow his way.

The night was young, thought Basheer Koya as he entered his compound. There was plenty of time to celebrate his success with his men. Faisal's friends could wait.

'This is crazy,' said Aditya, shutting the room door behind him. 'Faisal gone. He would never leave without telling us.'

'It is weird,' said Vikram. 'I can't believe it.' He surveyed the room. 'Look. All his stuff is lying here. He's taken nothing with him.' Vikram went over to Faisal's travel bag. Reaching inside, he plucked out a small book with Arabic inscriptions on it. It was Faisal's prayer book. 'Something's wrong,' said Vikram, handing the book to Aditya. 'Faisal would never have left his prayer book behind.'

Vikram collapsed on the bed. Aditya sat beside him, shoulders drooping. They stared out of the window, confused and too tired to speak.

'I don't like his uncle,' said Aditya, finally. 'And his friends are no better. I'm not looking forward to living here with him. If our trip gets cancelled tomorrow, we will move to Shaukat's place. Now that Faisal isn't here, we have no reason to stay on.'

Vikram nodded in agreement. 'Yeah, we'll go to Shaukat's. Mr Koya will be happy to be rid of us.'

The boys took turns at washing up. Ismail brought their dinner, which turned out to be surprisingly delicious.

'Basheer Koya must love his food,' said Aditya appreciatively as he dug into his meal. They thanked Ismail when he returned to collect their plates. Both boys decided to turn in. They needed a good night's sleep for an early start the next day—weather permitting, of course.

ESCAPE

Faisal was uncomfortable. That muscle-brained Ismail had fastened the ropes tight enough to restrain a horse. *He must have drawn great pleasure from his work too*, thought Faisal sourly. But worse than the ropes, it was the handkerchiefs stuffed in his mouth that troubled him. His jaws ached from the unaccustomed angle the intruding cloth forced him to keep them at.

Faisal was in the room beside the hall, exactly below the one Vikram, Aditya and he slept in. Faisal was familiar with the room. He had been put up there on earlier visits and hadn't enjoyed the experience. It was a dismal corner of the house with just one window and the only furniture was a bed, a chair and a cupboard. Ismail and his uncle had strapped him to the chair and for good measure, they had fastened the chair to the cupboard.

It was only because of the light entering from the curtained window that Faisal could keep track of the passage of time. For a long while, the glow in the room had stayed constant. Shortly after it started to fade, Ismail had entered with food and water. When Ismail plucked the handkerchiefs from his mouth, Faisal celebrated the release of his tongue by insulting him with a flow of colourful language. The caretaker did not take kindly to Faisal's verbal onslaught. He jammed the handkerchiefs back into Faisal's mouth and stalked out of the room.

The glow in the window had dimmed considerably when Faisal heard the sound of laughter from the hall. His uncle's friends had arrived.

His uncle had spoken of a celebration before locking him up in the room. 'You dirty little meddler,' he had said. 'You aren't going to stop me. Neither you nor your interfering father. I have achieved the impossible. I have kidnapped Kumar from right under the noses of the navy. We are going to drink and feast tonight. You're not going to spoil our merrymaking. I'll deal with you and your friends tomorrow.'

Loud voices indicated that the party had begun. Although Faisal could hear them, he couldn't make out the words they spoke. There were two doors between his room and the hall. Together, they muffled the babble of voices and revelry.

Some time later, fresh sounds from above alerted Faisal to Vikram and Aditya's return. The ceiling creaked as the boys shuffled around.

Despair overcame Faisal. His friends were here, just one floor above, yet he couldn't alert them of his presence. Faisal strained at his ropes. He tugged, he pulled, he wriggled, but to no avail. He worked his mouth, striving to dislodge the handkerchiefs wedged there. He exhaled hard, he pushed with his tongue. Gathering air in his lungs, he shouted, but the sound that emerged was soft, like a dog's whimper.

Faisal breathed hard. What could his friends be thinking? Would they believe his uncle's story? Faisal doubted they would. They weren't that stupid.

Time passed. The sounds from above ceased, indicating his friends had fallen asleep. Talk and laughter still streamed from the hall. His uncle's party was in full flow.

Faisal speculated on his uncle's plans for him. Basheer Koya had said that he would hold Faisal prisoner until the mission was successfully completed. But then what? Basheer Koya could not release him. Faisal was realistic enough to admit that he knew too much. What would happen then? Would he keep him a prisoner or would he dispose of him? Faisal shuddered. His past experiences with his uncle had taught him that the man was capable of doing anything—even murdering his own nephew.

The chilling possibility set Faisal straining at his bonds again. But he tired quickly. Faisal's head drooped. This wasn't working. He was wasting his efforts. He would have to try something else.

While he rested, Faisal studied the ropes that restrained him. He was strapped to a chair and the chair was fastened to a cupboard. The chair was immobile, and so was he. But even though his body and thighs were roped to the chair, his feet were free. *To what purpose*, thought Faisal, idly swinging his feet back and forth— they couldn't possibly help him break free.

The bed was nearby and Faisal noticed that when his feet were at full stretch, his toes grazed the edge of the bed. Faisal stared intently at the bed. *Was it possible?* he wondered. If he stretched his legs, could he hook his toes under it and pull it closer? The bed had an iron frame. It was heavy. Faisal's heart beat faster. What if he squeezed his toes under the bed railing and lifted it off the ground? Wouldn't it make a loud sound when he dropped it? Yes, it would. Would the noise alert Vikram and Aditya? Faisal had no answer to this, but even the flimsiest of possibilities was enough to get him started.

Faisal lengthened his legs, stretching them as far as he could. His toes grazed the bed railing and swung past it. He tried again and again, but his feet kept sailing past the bed. He could not hook his toes beneath its frame. *Maybe if he slid lower in the chair*, thought Faisal. He wrestled the ropes, trying to slide downwards. It wasn't easy. Ismail's handiwork held him fast to the chair. Faisal worked hard. But his breathing limited his efforts. The oxygen entering his chest wasn't enough. The handkerchiefs were the problem. They sealed his mouth and the supply that trickled through his nostrils wasn't adequate to sustain his exertions.

Yet Faisal persevered. After a Herculean struggle, punctuated by breathless pauses, his feet slid a couple of inches lower. When he swung them forward, they clasped the bed railing and he pulled it closer. Faisal collapsed on the chair, every muscle in his body aching.

Faisal rested. The sound of merriment filtered into the room. If anything, the revelry was even louder now.

Faisal stared at the bed. It was heavy. Lifting it was going to demand all his strength. Drawing a deep breath, he slid downwards in the chair, stretching as far as he could. His toes hooked easily beneath the frame. He strained his legs upwards. The bed barely rose from the ground. Faisal sweated silently. He grunted and doubled his efforts, pouring all his energy into the task. This time, the bed rose several inches off the ground. Faisal kept the bed suspended while he rested. He laboured at the cloth stuffed inside his mouth. He felt like a fish plucked from the sea, struggling to breathe. His ankles hurt so bad that he thought they might snap any moment. Faisal lifted again. The bed rose high off the ground. At the peak of his efforts, he let his legs go limp, releasing the bed in mid-air. It came crashing down with a loud thump.

The thump travelled through to the hall, but it did not disturb the occupants who had been drinking steadily through the evening. Both Vikram and Aditya, however, heard the muffled thump.

'Hopefully that's Ismail getting his head beaten up by Mr Koya,' said Aditya, yawning.

Vikram grinned in the darkness. He had been unable to sleep. Faisal's abrupt departure had left him deeply disturbed. Basheer Koya's story just didn't sound right. Vikram couldn't recollect any ferryboat leaving from the jetty. Ferryboats are large and he would have seen one if it had docked at the jetty. In any case, Shaukat's place was a short distance from there. Surely Faisal would have stopped by before leaving. And besides, there was a helicopter flight scheduled for the next day. Why depart on a long sea journey when he could reach home in an hour?

Vikram had come to the conclusion that Faisal had not left Kalpeni. The boy was somewhere on the island. His prayer book in the room was evidence enough. Basheer Koya had lied to them.

Vikram raised himself in his bed and looked at Aditya. 'You awake?' he asked.

Dim light from the street trickled into the room. Earlier, a sickle moon had cast a faint light on the island, but it had set long before.

'Yeah.' Aditya yawned. 'Can't sleep.' He rolled over and faced Vikram. 'We should tell Shaukat to cancel the trip tomorrow. What with the possibility of a storm and now Faisal's departure? I don't think we should be traipsing about enjoying ourselves while one of his relatives is terminally ill. I mean, we are his guests, aren't we?'

'True,' said Vikram. 'It's a shame, but yes, we should cancel the trip.' Vikram turned silent. He stared at Aditya's shaggy profile, unsure about airing his speculations. Then he spoke up. 'Something's going on,' he said. 'There's no way Faisal would ever abandon us. I don't believe Basheer Koya. He is a liar. Faisal is on this island. I am sure of it.'

Aditya's eyes grew wide.

Vikram explained his thoughts.

'I don't know,' said Aditya when Vikram was done. He looked doubtful. 'Why would his uncle lie to us? And if Faisal is here on this island, where is he?'

Vikram shrugged. 'No idea. But he is here, on Kalpeni.'

They were silent for a while, each occupied with his thoughts.

Aditya stretched. 'If what you say is true, Faisal is being held against his will. Left to himself, Faisal would be right here with us rather than anywhere else on the island.'

'Exactly. He is being held against his will. He could be anywhere on this island, maybe even right here in this . . .'

Vikram was cut off by yet another thump.

The sound seemed to have travelled up from the room below theirs. The boys looked at each other.

'That's the second time,' said Vikram. 'Do you think . . .' He left the sentence unfinished.

They were both out of their beds in a flash. Aditya was the first to the door. Pushing it open, he poked his head out. Light streamed from the hall into the yard, illuminating it. There was no one below. Aditya stepped out, signalling Vikram to follow. They crept silently down the stairs.

On reaching the ground, they crossed to the room below theirs, halting beside a solitary window with two shutters. The shutters were closed and a curtain was drawn behind them. The room was dark and unlit.

Vikram signalled Aditya to wait. He tapped lightly on a windowpane and placed his ear against it, listening intently. He heard a rustling inside. Furniture creaked.

'There's someone in there,' he whispered.

Vikram ran his fingers along the window, searching for an opening. The shutters were old and distorted. If he had something long and thin, he could insert it and pry open the latch. 'Get your penknife,' he whispered to Aditya.

Aditya slipped back to the room and returned with his knife. Vikram, meanwhile, had selected the more distorted and rickety frame. He placed his hand on one frame, pushing it. With his other hand, he pulled the distorted frame outwards, creating an opening. Aditya unhooked his penknife and inserted the blade through the opening. He ran it upwards till it touched the latch and then yanked hard. The latch slid out of the hole. Working quickly, they opened the second latch in a similar fashion.

The window swung open. Vikram pulled the curtain aside. The room was dark. A musty smell floated out. His eyes soon adjusted to the darkness. Inside, there was a bed and a cupboard. Both boys spotted a chair. Someone was sitting on it.

Aditya pulled himself into the room. Vikram followed. They found Faisal on the chair, his mouth propped open in an unnatural manner.

Vikram yanked the handkerchiefs from Faisal's mouth. Faisal's jaws finally loosened, but with excruciating pain. Although he tried, he was unable to speak. Vikram poured water from a bedside jug and fed it to Faisal.

'That swine of an uncle of mine,' hissed Faisal, after consuming a glass. 'Do you know what he's done? He's kidnapped the Tamilian from Sri Lanka. The one being protected by the navy at Kadmat.'

'Take it easy,' whispered Vikram while Aditya set about cutting Faisal's bonds.

Vikram fed Faisal another glass of water. The boys were so immersed in their task that they did not notice that the party sounds from the hall had ceased.

The sound of a door opening startled them. Vikram froze. Faisal's eyes rolled in panic. Aditya frantically cut away at Faisal's bonds.

'Run for it,' breathed Faisal. 'Head to the police station. Tell them my uncle has kidnapped Kumar from Kadmat. Say that he is being held on his boat at the jetty. The police must act tonight because they will be taking him away tomorrow to Tinakara Island. That's where they are going to hand him over to the militants.'

'Shut up,' hissed Aditya. 'We're not leaving without you.' Most of the bonds had been cut. Only the ones binding Faisal's thighs remained.

Footsteps pounded in the corridor, halting outside the door. Vikram cast a desperate look at Aditya who was furiously working on Faisal's bonds.

'Who's inside?' Basheer Koya pounded his fists on the door. 'Faisal, who's inside with you?' He shouted at Ismail, who was fumbling at the door. 'Quickly, you idiot. Open it quickly!'

Vikram's eyes swept the room. They settled on the water pitcher. It was a heavy earthen jar. He snatched it from the table and faced the door.

The door crashed open just as Aditya cut Faisal's final bond.

Ismail charged into the room. A few steps behind were Basheer Koya and his cronies.

Vikram flung the jar at Basheer Koya. Moving quickly, he stuck a leg between Ismail's feet, sending him crashing to the ground.

Meanwhile, Aditya had hauled Faisal out of the chair and had flung him out of the window. Aditya followed, leaping and landing in the yard beside Faisal.

Vikram paused for a moment, observing his handiwork. The pitcher had hit Basheer Koya on his chin and had then crashed to the ground where it had shattered. The impact of the pitcher had toppled Basheer Koya. He had tumbled backwards into his men, bringing them down with him. The water from the pitcher had flooded the floor and the men were scrabbling about in the mess. Ismail too was on the ground.

Vikram turned and leapt, joining his friends.

Outside, the situation was grim. Aditya was looking despairingly at Faisal.

The islander was on his feet, but his legs were buckling beneath him.

'Come on,' implored Aditya, dragging Faisal forward.

But Faisal's legs weren't responding. They had stiffened after half a day of immobility.

'Damn it, Faisal, don't fall,' shouted Aditya, grabbing at his friend.

Vikram looked back. There was commotion inside the room. It was only a matter of time before somebody emerged.

'I can't move,' sobbed Faisal. 'Leave me. You two have to go. Inform the police. You can rescue me later. Go!'

The window crashed open as the first of the men leapt through it. Vikram stared in anguish at Faisal.

Faisal settled the matter by flinging himself to the ground. 'GO!' he cried.

They had no choice now but to abandon Faisal. The boys sprinted to the fence. Leaping over it, they landed in soft sand.

'Make for the jetty,' shouted Vikram.

He looked back as they sprinted down the beach. There were two men chasing and a third had just leapt the fence. Vikram's feet slipped in the soft sand. He steered Aditya to the waterline where it was wet and firm. They ran faster, pulling ahead of their pursuers.

It was late. Vikram searched the beach for people, but there was not a soul to be seen. The islanders had turned in for the night.

The quiet of the night was broken by shouts behind them. There were answering calls from ahead. Vikram's throat turned dry. Not only were they being chased, but there were men ahead too.

Vikram looked around him as he ran. On his left, there was a straggly line of fences. The sea stretched to his right. The jetty loomed ahead. Evenly spaced tube lights illuminated it to its farthest tip out at sea.

Vikram looked ahead in despair. Beyond the jetty, three men were sprinting towards them. Behind, their pursuers were hot on their trail. Their only route was the jetty.

Aditya's thinking was identical to Vikram's. He was already pounding down the jetty. Vikram followed.

They raced past the boats tied alongside. Vikram looked ahead, staring in despair at the wall where the jetty ended. They were trapped. The men behind had seen that the boys were cornered. They had halted. They stood at the foot of the jetty, waiting for their comrades to catch up.

Vikram watched the men. 'Looks like we've had it,' he panted.

Aditya snorted. 'I'm not going to stand here and give in.' He turned, looking about him. 'We can jump into the water and swim away. They won't find us in the dark.'

Vikram had considered the idea and discarded it. The men were far better swimmers, and besides, some of the boats docked here might belong to Basheer Koya. They would be chased down in minutes.

A thought came to him. *How about their boat, the* Alisha? *It was docked at the end of the jetty. Maybe . . .*

A voice suddenly called out. 'What are you two doing here so late?'

The boys turned, not believing their ears.

'Something wrong?' continued the voice. It was coming from one of the boats. 'You both look like you've seen a ghost.'

Shaukat! He was on board the *Alisha*. They dashed to the jetty wall. Shaukat stood in the boat, hands on his hips, staring at them.

'The weather is bothering me,' continued Shaukat, scratching his head. 'We might have to cancel the trip. I've come down for some last-minute checks.'

The islander suddenly shouted. 'Hey!' he yelled. 'Take it easy, you'll hurt yourselves!'

The boys had leapt into the boat.

'Start the boat,' shouted Aditya. 'Let's go!'

'Take it easy,' protested Shaukat, when Aditya grabbed and swung him around.

Basheer Koya's men were yelling and pounding down the jetty.

Shaukat went rigid. Moments later, he broke into smooth, quick action.

'Untie the rope,' he instructed Vikram as he made for the motor. He grabbed the starter handle and twirled it with a practised jerk. The motor sprang to life.

The men were closing in. Vikram fiddled with the knots but to no avail. Shaukat crossed to Vikram's side. With two quick tugs, the rope came loose. He sprang back to the motor.

The first of the men was almost on them.

Shaukat engaged the motor and opened the throttle wide. The boat shot forward just as one of the men leapt from the jetty. They heard a startled yell as the man landed with a splash into the water.

'Yahoo!' yelled Aditya in sheer delight as Shaukat turned the boat in a wide arc from the jetty.

THE LAGOON

The jetty lights receded behind them. The island was a long dark shadow with pinpricks of light scattered along its length. A warm wind swept their faces as the boat sped a course parallel to the shore.

'Where should we go?' Shaukat had to shout over the clamour of the engine.

'To the police station,' yelled Vikram. 'Or anywhere on the coast where we can hide from these men.' He was looking back at the jetty as he spoke. Boat engines were roaring to life there.

A shadow shot forward from the jetty, its wake flashing in the black waters of the lagoon. It was quickly followed by two more shadows. Three trails of shimmering wakes streaked towards them. The *Alisha* reverberated from stem to stern as Shaukat opened the throttle as wide as he could.

Shaukat looked back. The first boat was gaining on them. The other two were bigger and slower. The speedboat was piloting a course between the *Alisha* and the island. Its objective was clear. It was cutting them off from the shore. Shaukat considered his options. It wasn't possible to make for the shore. The speedboat would intercept them before they could get there. The two bigger boats were charting a course between the *Alisha* and the reef. The slower boats weren't an immediate threat, but the faster one was. Shaukat turned the wheel. The *Alisha* veered away from the speedboat. It was now moving away from the island, towards the coral reef.

Vikram and Aditya hung on to the sunroof poles as the *Alisha* ploughed forward. Vikram's eyes were drawn to the sparkling phosphorescent trail of their wake. Three more trails snaked behind the boats chasing them.

Vikram searched the lagoon for fishermen. There could be some who were out on a night catch or laying nets. But its waters were dark and empty. They would have to fend for themselves. Even as Vikram watched, the speedboat changed course, heading straight for them.

Shaukat saw the boat change direction too. The pilot's plan was obvious. Their access to the shore had been cut. Now he intended to corner the *Alisha* against the reef.

The *Alisha* was racing in an arc between the curving reef and the island. The exit channel lay ahead. Shaukat could see the buoys marking it. On her current course, the *Alisha* would pass inside the first buoy. Shaukat looked back at the speedboat. The trajectory it had chosen would cross their path just beyond the second buoy. They would be intercepted within minutes.

Shaukat's head was spinning. Just minutes ago, he had been looking forward to a good night's sleep. Now he was speeding down the lagoon trying to dodge boats hell-bent on hunting him down.

But Shaukat had no intention of tamely giving up. He looked back at the speedboat. On its present bearing, it would trap the *Alisha* against the reef. His only hope was to head out between the exit buoys, into the open sea. But he would have to be careful. If the speedboat realized his intention, it could easily change course and prevent the *Alisha* from exiting.

Shaukat informed the boys about his plan. 'I'm heading out to sea,' he shouted. 'I have no choice. The boat's moving too fast. We don't stand a chance inside the lagoon.'

Aditya crossed to the boat's hold and rummaged inside. He emerged with an engine crank rod and a harpoon spear in his hands. He handed the rod to Vikram.

The speedboat was creeping up on them. Shaukat looked out at the reef. The exit buoys weren't far.

The bow of the speedboat cut forward, displacing arcs of glowing phosphorescent water. There were five men on board, some carrying weapons. Aditya tightened his grip on his harpoon spear.

The first buoy loomed out of the darkness. They were now speeding across the exit channel. The water turned choppy. Vikram and Aditya held on to the sunroof posts as the *Alisha* heaved and bucked. Waves thundered as they broke on the reef. The engine of the speedboat roared louder. Shaukat gripped the wheel tightly. There were dangerous coral formations here. He had to be careful. If he mistimed his turn, he would wreck his boat on them.

'Hold on!' shouted Shaukat. He glanced at the speedboat. It was scudding across the water, cutting into their path. He would have to turn soon. He eased his speed. The timing of the turn—he would have to get it right. Only after the speedboat passed the second buoy, when it would be too late for it to follow them. Shaukat searched for the second buoy. The speedboat was fast approaching it. This was the moment! He jammed down hard on the wheel, using all his strength.

The *Alisha* swerved violently.

'Hang on!' yelled Shaukat.

A wave washed over the boat, stopping the *Alisha* in its tracks. The wheel was almost wrenched from Shaukat's hands. He hung on grimly, holding the *Alisha* on course. They had passed out of the exit channel, but the danger was far from over. They still had to negotiate the channel waves. The boys watched as a wall of water moved swiftly towards them. Shaukat straightened the *Alisha*, pointing her straight at the surging mountain of water. A deafening roar tore at their ears as, with breathtaking speed, the *Alisha* mounted the wave and dropped behind it. The sea boiled and foamed as the next wave raced towards them. The boat sailed high again and was dumped once more.

The waves fell behind them and soon they were in the swells of the open sea.

Shaukat scanned the water, searching for the boats pursuing them. He expected the speedboat to resume the chase, but there was no sign of it. The swells of the ocean obscured his vision. Only when they topped a swell could he look inside the reef. He spotted two boats. They were the bigger, slower ones. Of the speedboat, there was no sign. One of the big boats had come to a halt. The other was nosing the area where Shaukat had sprung his sudden turn.

Occupied with their exit from the lagoon, the boys hadn't witnessed the action behind them. On seeing their unexpected turn out of the channel, the pilot of the speedboat had attempted the same. In the heat of the moment, he took the turn without thinking. Because of his elevated speed, he was forced to take a wider turn. The broad sweep brought him to the coral outcroppings and he smashed into them. His speed was such that the speedboat tore apart on impact.

Shaukat could find no sign of the speedboat. Vikram and Aditya stood beside him, searching the frothy waters of the exit channel.

'Where on earth is it?' asked Aditya.

Vikram scratched his head. 'It's done a ghost trick and vanished.'

Shaukat turned a full circle, scanning the lagoon, the reef, the exit channel and the ocean. The two bigger boats were clearly visible. But the speedboat had disappeared. It was the boat searching the area where he had taken the turn that provided Shaukat the clue.

'The speedboat is gone,' he announced. 'Wrecked. It must have hit the reef at full speed.'

Vikram's eyes grew wide. 'Do you think the boat is destroyed?' he asked.

'Remember how fast it was travelling. Coral is hard, like rock. At that speed, the coral must have torn the boat into two.'

The boys looked at each other. They smiled hesitantly, unsure. They cast glances at the exit channel, half-expecting the speedboat to emerge from the darkness and dash their hopes. But no such thing happened. All they saw was the bobbing lights of the other boats.

Shaukat turned to the boys. 'May I know what's going on?' he asked. 'I have been chased like a thief. I have risked my life and my boat. Can someone please tell me why?'

Aditya's teeth flashed in the dark. He grinned. 'It's all Faisal's fault,' he said.

Shaukat stared at him.

Vikram spoke sharply. 'This is not the time for playing the fool, Aditya.' He turned to Shaukat. 'It's a long story. We don't have the time for it now. We still have to get away from them.' He pointed at the boats. 'Tell me, is there another entrance to the lagoon?'

Shaukat shook his head and said, 'Not on this side of the island. There is one on the other side, but it is unmarked and dangerous. You can't use it at night. We can't re-enter the lagoon until those boats go away.'

Vikram pursed his lips in thought. 'Does that mean—'

But Aditya suddenly interrupted. 'Look,' he cried, pointing behind them.

Two boats were exiting the lagoon. The boats separated, one making for their left, the other striking out to their right. It was obvious what they were up to.

The chase was on!

NIGHT RUN

It was a clear, moonless night that gave not even the slightest hint of the storm to come. The sky was spattered with stars. The Milky Way arched across the sky—silken and luminous. But just as the sky was ablaze, the sea was dark and forbidding. Deep swells rode its surface. The *Alisha* trailed a fiery green wake that was easily visible to her pursuers.

The shapeless shadow of Kalpeni had shrunk and disappeared long since. The boats chasing them had doused their lights. Yet, even in the dark of the night, they were visible: two smudges on the far horizon. By now it was clear that the *Alisha* was not capable of losing her pursuers. Shaukat had been powering her at full speed the past few hours, yet the boats had held fast behind them, always visible, like wolves tailing their prey.

The *Alisha* had been moving in a southerly direction. Though Shaukat had a compass, he steered by the stars. When he was a boy, his grandfather would take him out to sea at night, pointing out the stars and the constellations. When Shaukat had learnt them, he would challenge him to steer the boat back to Kalpeni in the dark. Now the heavens and its millions of stars were familiar territory. The constellations were old friends and by noting their height and location, he could tell exactly where he was.

At the present moment, he was steering a course towards the Tinakara-Pitti Islands. The wind had picked up the past hour, convincing Shaukat that a storm was on its way. Shaukat had evaluated the probability of the *Alisha* surviving a storm on the open sea, and had concluded that the odds were not in their favour. They would have to seek shelter on land. Although still far away, the Tinakara-Pitti Islands were their best hope. There was enough time to make it to the islands. They could ride out the storm there and return after it had passed.

At the start of the chase, Shaukat had considered staying put in the vicinity of Kalpeni. *Alisha* wasn't a speedboat, but neither were the bigger boats pursuing them. He could have managed to dodge them. Then he had remembered that Basheer Koya owned several boats. If more boats joined the chase, they would have been cornered and run down. So he had turned away from Kalpeni and since the Tinakara-Pitti Islands were the nearest refuge in case of a storm, he had steered south. But Shaukat didn't want to reveal his plan to his pursuers. So he kept changing course in an apparently aimless manner. He hoped that his ploy would fool them into thinking that his only intention was to escape them and that he had no destination in mind.

Shaukat had explained his plans to the boys and had sought their view.

Aditya had placed an arm around Shaukat. 'You know best,' he had said.

The boys had then recounted the events of the evening.

Shaukat had been immensely saddened by their story. 'Kidnapping!' He had spat the word out. 'It doesn't happen here on the islands. It is an ill of the mainland. Faisal's uncle is ruining our reputation. We islanders are God-fearing, honest and law-abiding citizens. Murders are unheard of. Even simple crimes like robbing and cheating don't take place here. We take pride in not troubling our police. They have no work because hardly any crimes are committed here. And Basheer Koya does this?' Shaukat had hung his head. Then he had pointed at the boats behind. 'Now he's trying to kill us.'

The boys had remained silent. They understood Shaukat's feelings. It was a shame that Basheer Koya belonged to these islands.

The insistent throb of the engine numbed their ears. The *Alisha* was like a roller-coaster machine, pitching and rolling and tossing them about. It was positively dangerous on the deck. A lapse in concentration, however fleeting, could result in being swept out into the sea. Vikram fingered the life jacket he wore. Shaukat had handed jackets to them earlier. But they did not inspire confidence. The waves were climbing higher each minute. He doubted whether they would save them in this kind of a sea.

Time passed.

The two smudges hovered behind them, trailing luminescent wakes. Clouds appeared. They were small and they scudded across the skies, blotting out the stars. The *Alisha* throbbed along, Shaukat standing impassively at the wheel. The swells were running longer and deeper. Often, when they topped a swell and hurtled down the other side, the next swell would swing across their bows and dump water on them. The boys bailed the boat every few minutes.

Then a terrifying incident took place.

Aditya had been gaining confidence with each bailing operation. His movements had quickened. He travelled twice as fast as Vikram, balancing adroitly, anticipating the rolling of the boat and adjusting his weight to its tilt. But in doing so, he made himself vulnerable to rogue waves that could strike the boat without warning. On one of his trips with the bailing bucket, an unexpected wave caught the *Alisha* sideways. Unbalanced at that moment, Aditya's feet were jerked from under him. The next thing he knew, he was flying across the boat. He saved himself from being carried overboard by clinging to one of the sunroof poles.

Shaukat summoned the boys to the wheel. The islander had never displayed anger before, but on this occasion, his chin was trembling. 'We are not in a lagoon,' he shouted. 'This is the deep sea and a storm wind is blowing. If either of you go overboard, that will be the end. Turning the boat around can take forever. By that time, the waves would have carried you away. I will never be able to find you. Any man overboard is a dead man. Remember that.' He glowered at Aditya. 'No heroics. This is not a movie. It's life and death out here.'

Aditya was a chastened boy. When he bailed the boat next, he crawled on hands and knees. Vikram, too, moved slower and with extreme caution.

Later, while clouds filled the skies, Vikram crossed to the hold. He was thirsty. Crouching, he opened its doors and unhitching the torch clamped there, he turned it on and flashed it inside. He spotted cans of food and bottles of water. They rolled with the motion of the boat. There were other provisions stashed inside. He saw large jerrycans. Some were filled with water, others smelled of petrol. *Bless Shaukat and his meticulous planning*, thought Vikram. There was enough fuel to travel to the Tinakara-Pitti Islands and back. The windsurf boards Aditya and he had used were strapped tightly in the well of the boat.

After drinking his fill, Vikram handed Aditya and Shaukat a bottle each.

'When do you think the storm will hit us?' he asked Shaukat.

Shaukat looked up, studying the clouds. 'Not for a while. Could be late morning or the afternoon. But there's no need to worry. We should make it to the islands by then. In any case, we'll be upwind of the islands. If we don't make it and are caught out at sea, the wind will sweep us towards them.' He did not tell Vikram that if the storm hit them at sea, there was a likelihood of the *Alisha* being torn apart and none of them surviving.

'How long will the storm last?' asked Aditya.

Shaukat shrugged. 'Impossible to say. Could be a few hours, could be an entire day. My feeling is that it's going to be a big one. It's been flashing warning signals since yesterday.'

Vikram shivered. The waves had drenched them from head to toe and the wind was blowing. 'Our absence from Kalpeni will be noticed in the morning, won't it?' he asked.

Shaukat nodded. 'Sure it will, but I doubt if anyone is going to come searching for us. It won't be safe for boats to be out. They will wait for the storm to subside. The navy could send helicopters, but they will search in the wrong direction. Everybody is under the impression that we would be heading in the opposite direction—to the sandbanks. So don't count on outside help. We will have to look after ourselves.'

A knot formed in Vikram's stomach. They would have to battle the storm on their own.

'Will the boats pursue us during the storm?' asked Aditya.

Shaukat shook his head. 'It's every man for himself. They will abandon us before the storm breaks. They are pushing us away from Kalpeni. When they feel we are too far to return, they will make a run for Kalpeni.'

'Why don't we turn back for Kalpeni too?' asked Aditya.

Shaukat turned and pointed to the smudges. 'That's why.'

'But once they abandon us, can't we also follow to Kalpeni?'

'I'm not going to risk it. The *Alisha* is old and not as sturdy as their boats. I don't want to be caught halfway in a storm. The Tinakara-Pitti Islands are a better bet. We can sit out the storm and head back after it has passed.'

Shaukat fell silent. The boys resumed their bailing duty.

Above them clouds flocked the sky, extinguishing the fiery pinpricks of the stars till nothing but a black emptiness covered the heavens. Now only one smudge followed them; the other had disappeared into the night.

Shaukat called out to the boys. 'Only one boat now,' he said. 'The other one has dropped out.'

Vikram and Aditya searched the waters behind them.

'When do you think the remaining one will turn around?' asked Aditya.

Shaukat looked out across the water. 'If I was the captain of that ship, I'd chase till I was sure that the *Alisha* has no chance of returning to Kalpeni before the storm breaks. That would be an hour or two at the most. Our present bearing is twenty degrees east of the Tinakara-Pitti Islands. I'm giving the impression that I don't know where the islands are. But the moment they leave, I will head for them.'

Presently, a watery glow appeared on the eastern horizon. It turned a dull grey and crept across the sky. Clouds hung like a soggy blanket overhead. The sea beneath them was a menacing grey, tipped with fast-moving frothy flecks. It was a forbidding dawn, cold and wet and frightening. Vikram shivered as he searched for their pursuers. Visibility was poor, his vision hampered by the waves towering around them. Only during the brief moments when they crested a wave was he able to see any distance. He searched and searched the horizon, but there was no sign of their pursuers.

SHIPWRECK

Vikram nudged Shaukat and pointed behind them.

Shaukat handed the wheel to Vikram and surveyed the horizon. The islander's eyes were sharper than Vikram's. The sea was empty. There was not a boat to be seen.

'Good news,' he announced. 'There's nobody following us.' He turned silent for a moment, thinking. 'This can mean one of two things. They could have lost us in the dark. That's possible. But I don't think that is the case. It's more likely that they have abandoned the chase. Their mission was done. They pushed us far from Kalpeni. Too far to make it back before the storm strikes.'

'So what do we do now?' asked Aditya who had joined them.

'We make for Tinakara at full speed. We have to get there before the storm breaks.'

Vikram returned the wheel to Shaukat. The islander consulted his compass and turned the boat to port. Neither Vikram nor Aditya had any clue where the islands lay. They were both dependent on Shaukat and his abilities as a sailor. *But things couldn't have worked out better*, thought Vikram.

If he had to choose anyone to entrust his life to on the high seas, he would unhesitatingly select Shaukat.

The *Alisha* ploughed on. In the massive emptiness of the sea, she was a toy, insignificant, inconsequential—a plaything of the waves. They battered her, they tossed her, they shook her from stem to stern. Somehow she managed to climb each wave, though sometimes only just. The moment she sank down the far side of a swell, the leading edge of the next wave would tower mountain-like over her. Sometimes as she crested a wave, its upper part would break on her bow, showering the boys with frothing saltwater. On occasions when the wave was monstrous, it would strike the *Alisha* with appalling force. Vikram's legs were often swept away under him and only his clinging hands saved him from being swept overboard.

Vikram turned, searching for his friends. Aditya was on the opposite side of the wheel from where he sat, wedged comfortably between the upraised wheel stand and the bow of the boat. Shaukat stood at the wheel, water streaming from his face. His carefully combed hair was a mess, clumped like seaweed on his head.

Aditya caught Vikram's eye and waved. There was a big grin on his face. Vikram had seen that grin before. It was a sign that Aditya was enjoying himself. At one level, the ride was exhilarating. Cresting the waves and shooting down the other side was loads of fun. But at the same time, the sea was frightening and there was no hiding from the certainty that a storm was on its way. Their lives could be in danger. Vikram could not ignore these thoughts.

But Aditya could. The sea was tempestuous. Aditya was enjoying its challenge.

The morning wore on. The sky remained unchanged— a uniformly dull grey. They managed a bite of soggy biscuits that Aditya extracted from the hold. Vikram wondered if the *Alisha* was making any significant progress. He asked Shaukat when they would reach the islands.

'Soon.' Shaukat spoke tersely. 'Be patient.'

Vikram refrained from asking any further questions. The pressure on the islander was immense. He could see the whiteness on Shaukat's fingers where they grasped the wheel, holding on tightly—fighting the sea that was trying to wring it from his grasp.

Towards midday, the sky started to darken. Black cumulus clouds were massing in the skies. At the wheel, Shaukat was turning desperate. Where were the islands? If he did not spot them soon, they would be lost. By his calculations, they were to appear on the horizon any moment. Was he wrong?

The clouds covered the skies with frightening speed. Never before in his life had Vikram seen such dark clouds.

Shaukat anxiously scanned the horizon. The air had a thundery feel to it. Vikram watched in awe as flickers of lightning danced against the advancing blackness. The sea around them had turned a harsh silver, but under the thunderclouds, it was black. Aditya gulped. His exhilaration had long been washed away, displaced by dread and dismay.

This time, when they crested a wave, Shaukat's heart leapt with joy. He had spotted a shadow on the water.

The islands!

They were nearby. He hadn't seen them because he had been searching to starboard. They had appeared some time ago on his port side. He could see palm trees bent double in the wind. While he watched, a curtain of rain swept over the trees, moving rapidly towards the *Alisha*.

Shaukat shouted at the top of his voice. 'Land! I can see the islands!'

'Yay!' yelled the boys. Aditya whooped with delight. Vikram waved a fist in the air.

But the tension remained as the advancing black line moved closer.

The wind picked up, whistling itself to a frenzy. The rain swept across them with startling suddenness, enveloping them and blotting out all traces of the islands. But Shaukat had seen them once, and that was enough. The rain hissed down in torrents, hammering them with ferocious intensity. Jagged lines of lightning struck the sea like whiplashes. A clap of thunder exploded with stunning violence above them.

Shaukat struggled grimly with the wheel. The sea boiled and foamed angrily, pitching and rolling them at will. Vikram and Aditya hung on tight. If they lost their grip now, they would be lost forever.

The sky was putting on a breathtaking visual performance. Tongues of lightning flickered in all directions, some of them cracking into the water right next to them. It was a scene that could shake the heart of even the bravest sailor. Nature was displaying every weapon in her arsenal.

The sea had the *Alisha* in its grip. It flung her around with staggering violence. Shaukat could barely control the boat. It was all he could do to ensure that the *Alisha* met each wave head-on. Shaukat prayed. He begged Allah to sweep them to the islands. If they missed the islands, they were doomed.

The rain continued without letting up, cascading around them in thick curtains. Vikram's heart was in his mouth. It was obvious that Shaukat had lost control of the boat.

A wave hit them sideways, almost keeling the boat over. The *Alisha* valiantly righted herself, but only just. The next wave rose mountainously above her. The poor *Alisha* had no time to adjust herself before it struck. A huge wall of water broke over her, engulfing her with tons of hissing water. The sunroof walls collapsed, soundlessly splintering into fragments that were swept away with appalling swiftness. But the *Alisha* refused to go down, rising bravely over the next wave.

Vikram wondered how long the boat could take such a battering. She was bound to crumble under such a vicious onslaught. The waves were now sweeping across the boat with chilling regularity, lifting and flinging the boys around like toys. Vikram and Aditya hung on for all they were worth. Vikram's arms were numb with pain. His eyes were on fire—gritty salt had penetrated his eyeballs—he could hardly keep them open. He clung on, trying desperately to shut out his thoughts. But his mind refused. He kept wondering how the end would come. Would he lose his grip and be swept away? Or would the boat break up under them?

He suddenly noticed a change in the movement of the boat. They were no longer being tossed and turned by the waves; instead they seemed to be moving at a tremendous speed. For a fleeting moment, Vikram felt he was on a rollercoaster ride.

Shaukat had noticed the change in movement too. From his vantage point on the wheel, he could see why. They were in the grip of a mighty roller, which was moving at a frightening speed. Ahead he saw other rollers, all hurtling in the same direction. His heart lifted. The rollers could only mean one thing—they were being swept towards a coral reef. They were going to hit the islands! But he couldn't celebrate. Although the reef was their salvation, it was their greatest danger too. It would wreck the *Alisha*, rip her apart like a matchbox.

He waited till the roller released its hold on them. Before the next roller had them, he was down, telling the boys to prepare for a shipwreck.

'When the boat breaks up, don't cling to the wreckage,' he shouted. 'If a wave pushes you over the reef, don't struggle against it. Don't fight it. Let it carry you into the lagoon.'

He sprang back to the wheel. They were already in the grip of the next roller. Shaukat pulled hard on the wheel, trying to straighten the boat. He had to hit the reef head-on to minimize damage and lessen the likelihood of injuries. He watched the next roller build up around him. It was a long wave that stretched endlessly on both sides of the *Alisha*. He squinted in the streaming rain, searching for the reef. In the distance, he saw a foaming white line.

That was the reef all right. They were headed for it. They would strike it soon. Two, maybe three rollers would get them there. Shaukat waited for the inevitable.

The storm continued. Lightning flashed, thunder exploded and rain cascaded in stinging torrents. The reef drew closer. It was their saviour and also their destroyer. The surf was pounding across it with ghastly intensity. Shaukat shuddered at the thought of the damage the sharp edges of the submerged coral could inflict.

Soon, they were in striking distance of the reef. The next roller would cast them on to it.

Shaukat felt a roller clasp them in its unforgiving grip. He fought it, pointing the nose of the boat at the reef. They were moving like an express train now. The reef loomed closer and closer.

'This is it!' he shouted.

The *Alisha* straightened herself, rising to the occasion—looking as dignified as was possible with her broken sunroof—riding the surf bravely to certain destruction. She hit the reef head-on with a resounding crash. There was a loud screeching sound as her underside was ripped apart by the razor-sharp coral. The roller continued to push her, forcing her to swing sideways till she settled wearily on the reef. The sea receded on either side of her, leaving her beached for a moment before the next roller slammed into her, lifting her clear off the reef and flinging her in a broken heap into the lagoon.

On hearing Shaukat's warning shout, Vikram had steeled himself for the crash. He watched the creamy line of froth marking the reef approach rapidly. The impact was bone-jarring when it came. He knew that the hull had been ripped apart. He watched helplessly as the boat was lifted and deposited on the reef. His ears were deafened by the sound of ripping wood and pounding surf. Water poured into the boat. He couldn't see Aditya or Shaukat. It was every man for himself. He felt the next roller pound into the *Alisha*. Remembering Shaukat's advice, he loosened his grip on the *Alisha* and let himself be carried along by the wave. He was propelled head over heels, losing all sense of direction as he was cartwheeled along. He clamped his lips shut, preventing his mouth from being flooded with seawater. He felt a jarring thud on his shoulder. He was being dragged along something hard and grainy. He stuck his hands out to stop himself, but the wave continued to push him—tugging and tossing him before finally depositing him at the water's edge.

With a roar the water receded around him, pulling him back into the lagoon. He struggled in vain as the sea dragged him back into its furious midst. Vikram ceased to struggle as another wave drove him forward, hurling him on to hard unyielding sand before subsiding. He fought to raise himself, wrestling against the back draught of the receding wave. Like a drunken man, he staggered forward till he collapsed in shallow water. Rain streamed down in a solid grey curtain around him. Vikram had never felt so thoroughly soaked in his life. He sat lifelessly in the sand, staring vacantly at the sea, allowing the exhaustion and tension to seep from him. His numbed mind struggled to accept the fact that he was still alive.

'You okay?' shouted somebody in his ear. Aditya was staring down at him, a wide grin splitting his dripping face. Vikram smiled back at him.

Aditya pointed at the sea. A bedraggled figure was emerging from the dull fog of rain. Vikram's heart warmed at the sight of Shaukat trudging wearily towards them. This human was the sole reason they were still alive. Shaukat had risen magnificently to the occasion, triumphantly battling the sea and the storm. The victory had thoroughly drained the islander and he crumpled in an exhausted heap next to the boys.

They sat side by side in the pounding rain, staring sightlessly at the raging storm, letting their nervous energy seep from their exhausted minds, deliciously savouring the knowledge that they had survived.

MAROONED

The rain did not let up. It continued through the day and into the night. It was cold. The rain ensured they remained wet and there was no shelter from the wind on the island. Shaukat led them to an area at the edge of the palm trees and instructed them to dig pits in the sand. It was warmer inside the pits, he said, particularly when they spread sand over themselves.

Luckily, nourishment wasn't a problem. The storm had thrown down hundreds of coconuts and more fell as the wind continued to dislodge them from the trees. Shaukat expertly cracked them open with Aditya's penknife. The deliciously sweet water and chewy copra satisfied their thirst and hunger.

There was no twilight that evening. The murky sky simply turned dark. The night was long and cold and uncomfortable. Shafts of lightning illuminated the storm-battered island. The sea pounded thunderously against the reef. The wind howled and tore at the trees. Sometimes it cleaved them in two and the boys would hear a bullet-like retort as the hapless tree snapped and crashed

111

to the ground. The wind and the rain persisted through the night. The boys suffered in silence.

Dawn brought little respite. A wet glow appeared in the sky. A dull light spread across the lagoon and sea, revealing a world that was entirely grey. The sky was dark and grey. The waves lashing the shore were grey. The rain was grey. Even the sand on the beach reflected a sheen of grey.

Sleep was impossible. So the boys roused themselves and explored the island. Torn and twisted palm fronds lay in heaps on the sand. Scattered in their midst were uprooted trees and the broken remnants of trunks that the wind had snapped. Coconuts littered the sand, and strewn everywhere were clumps of seagrass that the sea had swept in. Only a handful of trees had survived the storm; they stood proud and tall, continuing their battle with the wind.

They found both the windsurf boards in the midst of the tangled debris. They had broken loose from the ill-fated *Alisha* and had been deposited on the island. Of the *Alisha*—except for fragments of broken wood—there was no sign.

'Poor *Alisha*,' sighed Vikram.

Shaukat picked up a scrap of wood from the sand. 'My *Alisha* was a brave boat. She battled the storm till the very end, falling apart only when she knew we were safe.' Shaukat swallowed. 'There won't be another boat like her . . .'

The boys bowed their heads in silence.

Finally, it was Aditya who spoke: 'Will we find the supplies stowed on her?'

Shaukat ran his fingers through his wet hair. 'I don't see why not,' he said. 'If her hold is still intact, the supplies will be inside her at the bottom of the lagoon. But if the hold has broken up—which is likely the case—then they will be scattered all over the place.'

Aditya scratched his stomach. 'Let's dive and retrieve whatever we can. I don't know about you guys, but I'm hungry.'

Shaukat shook his head. 'You can't dive in these conditions. It's dangerous in the lagoon. And even if you go under, it will be too murky to see anything. The earliest we can dive is tomorrow and that too, only if the storm lets up.'

Aditya stared. 'What do we do about food then?'

'Coconuts!' grinned Shaukat.

Aditya looked at him in disgust.

Vikram laughed.

The island was small and circular. At its widest, it was barely 100 metres across. This was Pitti Island, Shaukat informed them. Tinakara, the larger island, lay on the other side of the lagoon. They couldn't see it because of the rain.

They walked around Pitti, searching for pieces of wreckage. The gloomy conditions persisted, but the rain eased to a drizzle. They found both the windsurf masts. One had cracked into two, but the other was intact. They also found both jerrycans of water, still tied to one another, and much to Aditya's delight, several cans of baked beans and condensed milk.

Later they feasted on cold beans, condensed milk and coconut copra—a meal that Aditya surprisingly conceded as delicious. Soon the rain stopped altogether. Black rain clouds were replaced by a ceiling of brighter grey ones.

Vikram leaned back on a broken tree trunk. 'The people at Kalpeni must be wondering what happened to us,' he said.

Shaukat's face turned dark. 'My parents must be devastated. The last I spoke with them was after dinner, when I told them that I was going to the boat. There's no trace of the boat now, or of any of us, and a storm has struck.' Shaukat drew patterns on the wet sand. 'My father is a seaman. He must have given up all hope by now.'

'Hey,' said Aditya. 'Don't be so morbid. Think of it the other way. Just imagine their joy when they discover that we are alive and well.'

Vikram smiled.

Aditya tossed sand at a passing crab. 'My dad is the sort who can't keep still, particularly when he is stressed or unhappy. If I know him, he'll be out looking for us the minute he learns we're missing.'

Vikram turned his head to the sky. 'That's if the weather permits. I don't think anybody will be flying yet.'

Aditya scanned the skies too. 'You're right. Maybe not now. But he'll be itching to go. If the clouds keep clearing, he will be out searching.' He turned to Shaukat. 'Do you think Dad will find us?'

Shaukat sighed. 'I don't think so. We told everybody that we were headed north, to the sandbanks. The search will be conducted to the north of Kalpeni—not south, where we are.'

No one was going to come searching for them. It was a sobering thought, yet inexplicably a grin appeared on Vikram's face. 'I thought it only happened in the old days . . . but it's happened to us,' he said, his grin widening till it touched his eyes. 'Shipwrecked!' he cried, throwing his head back and raising his arms. 'We are shipwrecked on a coral island! Even in my wildest dreams, I could never have imagined this.'

Aditya's expression turned scornful. 'You can have this island and all that is on it, Vikram. This Robinson Crusoe stuff isn't for me. There's no fun in being stuck here for months on end with only coconuts to feed me.'

'Just think of it, Aditya. No school, no homework, no studies. Just sand, surf, coral and a beautiful lagoon.' Vikram's eyes shone. 'We can sail, we can surf and we can have the time of our lives. Isn't that what you always wanted?'

Aditya grunted. Put that way, their predicament did not appear so bad. 'Maybe you're right.' A grin appeared on his face, widening quickly till it was bigger even than Vikram's. 'I hate the first month of a new term. It's the worst. Enjoying the sun and the sand is far better than attending classes and . . . ugh, homework!'

They all laughed. Vikram jumped to his feet. 'Right,' he said. 'This is our new home. Let's explore.'

Aditya refused to get up. 'What's there to explore? We can walk around this place in minutes.'

'This is Pitti Island,' said Shaukat. 'It is the smaller of the two islands here. We don't have to live here. We can move to Tinakara, which is much bigger.'

Vikram halted in mid-stride. 'Wait a minute,' he said, turning to Aditya. 'Do you remember what Faisal said? He was babbling about Tinakara Island.'

Aditya scratched his head. 'Yes. Now that you mention it, I do recall him jabbering about these islands. To be honest, I wasn't paying attention. Ismail and Basheer Koya were at the door and I had to set Faisal free. My mind was on the ropes, but I do recollect him saying something about Tinakara.'

'I remember now,' said Vikram. 'It was about Basheer Koya and his men. They had kidnapped Kumar—the Tamil man from Sri Lanka. Faisal said that they were to bring Kumar to these islands. Their plan was to hand him over to the militants at Tinakara.'

Aditya stared at Vikram.

'Is this true?' asked Shaukat.

'It is,' said Vikram.

Shaukat turned to Aditya.

Aditya nodded. 'It's true, Shaukat. I don't remember exactly what Faisal said, but he was going on about militants and the police and Tinakara Island.' Aditya's face hardened. 'But who cares. Let them come. I have a thing or two to settle with that creep, Basheer Koya.'

'Sure you do, Aditya,' said Vikram. 'All of us do. More Shaukat than either of us. He's lost his boat because of Faisal's uncle. But let's be sensible about this. We are no match for Basheer Koya and his cronies. At this moment, all I can think of is that there are two islands. Maybe we can hide on one of them.'

'Yeah, sure you can,' sneered Aditya. 'And which one of the islands may I ask?'

'That's easy,' said Shaukat. 'They will land on Tinakara. Everyone does. It's a much bigger island and it also has a nice bay where you can anchor your boat. Pitti is very small and far too close to the reef. Also, there is no fresh drinking water on Pitti. Tinakara has plenty of water. If Mr Koya's men are coming here, they will choose Tinakara.'

Vikram looked relieved.

The islander rose to his feet and stretched. 'Can we discuss this later? No one's going to bother us for a while. Mr Koya and his men are not going to travel in the storm. They will have to sit it out.' Shaukat looked up. The sky was covered with clouds, but they were high, not the rain-bearing variety. 'The weather's easing up. Come on. Let's search the island. Useful stuff could have been washed ashore. More food cans too, Aditya.'

They searched the storm-battered island and gathered an hour later to take stock.

'Only five cans,' grumbled Aditya. 'Just five, and we'd bought so many.'

'Who cares,' said Vikram. 'Look at all the windsurf parts we've found.'

Shaukat was on his knees, sorting a pile of sand-crusted objects. 'We've been lucky with the boards,' he said. 'I can promise you one serviceable board tomorrow for sure. That will be fun. We'll all be able to sail.' He turned to Aditya. 'We'll find more of your precious food cans. They're underwater, inside the *Alisha*. We'll pull them out tomorrow.'

The only other items they had found were a coil of rope and a tarpaulin.

Vikram looked at the tarpaulin. 'Wish we had found it last night. It would have kept us warm.'

'True,' said Shaukat. 'I had packed it for the sandbanks. It will be useful here too.'

The boys were tired, having hardly slept the past two nights. After a meal of coconuts and canned food, they spread the tarpaulin on the beach and fell asleep. They slept deeply, through the afternoon and late into the evening. Above them, the clouds slowly dissipated. When Vikram woke, the setting sun had pierced the veil of clouds and had coloured the sky a fiery shade of red.

Vikram sprang up. The sun! It had been so long. He felt a deep desire to reach out and grab it. The sky was visible too. Bits of it, where there was no cloud. Everything was red. It was as if the heavens were ablaze. Vikram spread his hands outwards. Although feeble at this late hour, the sun still warmed his skin. He breathed deeply, savouring the moment.

'Beautiful, isn't it?' spoke a voice beside him. Shaukat was awake. He was sitting up, hands clasped to his knees, his face red in the sunlight. 'It's clearing up. Tomorrow should be nice and sunny.'

They sat companionably, enjoying the fireworks in the sky. Aditya lay between them, fast asleep.

Later, as the sun slipped into the sea, they took a walk around the island. On the far side of the beach, Shaukat pointed out Tinakara Island. It was long and flat and topped with palm trees. Set against the wide, darkening horizon, it looked ever so lonely and small. Vikram felt a flutter in his stomach. It struck him that they were alone— just the three of them on a tiny island, surrounded by emptiness. There was great beauty in the emptiness, but it was daunting too. Measured against it, he was insignificant, miniscule, no more than a grain of sand.

Shaukat knew how Vikram felt. Often, when he took his boat out to sea, he experienced the same humbling feeling.

They found Aditya awake and hungry when they returned. In the failing light, they consumed an early dinner. It was dark when they finished. A sickle moon hung low above the horizon and stars twinkled soggily in the heavens.

Aditya lay contentedly on the sand, gazing up at the stars. 'If this is what shipwrecked life is all about, it's not too bad,' he said.

Vikram stretched out beside Aditya. 'Can't get better,' he agreed.

Aditya yawned. 'I can get used to this. You're right, Vikram. This is the life.'

Vikram cupped his hands underneath his head. 'Everything seems so far away. School too. It's kind of unreal.'

'Hope it stays unreal,' said Aditya. 'Unreal for a long time. I want to enjoy this island.'

Vikram smiled. He thought drowsily about school. Missing a few weeks couldn't hurt. He too was looking forward to enjoying the island.

ADITYA AND THE REEF

The sun was shining through the trees when Vikram woke up. His heart soared as he looked at the sky. It was bright and blue and cloudless. All traces of the storm had cleared. He sat up. There was no sign of Shaukat and Aditya. He pulled himself to his feet. This was unusual—Aditya waking before him. Aditya was an incurably late riser. What could have motivated him to be up so early?

Vikram discovered why when he rounded a bend on the beach. Two heads bobbed in the lagoon waters, both wearing snorkelling masks. It was for the clear, bright water that Aditya had sacrificed his sleep.

Vikram waved.

One of the heads returned his greeting. It was Shaukat. He was pointing to the shore. Vikram looked. A pile of things were heaped at the water's edge. Vikram knelt beside them. Scattered on the sand were a mask, a box, a spear and food cans—objects from *Alisha*'s hold. Her wreck had been found.

Vikram wasted no time. Slipping on the salvaged mask, he stepped into the lagoon. The water was cool and refreshing and it had a rich, salty taste. Striking out, he soon reached the area where Aditya and Shaukat floated. He submerged himself and looked down.

The *Alisha*, or what remained of her, lay on a bed of sand, weighed down under several metres of water. Surprisingly, the boat was still in one piece. Sunlight rippled through the water, tracing patterns on her hull. A fish emerged from the boat. Pausing, it glanced at him and then swam away.

Drawing a deep breath, Vikram flipped his head into the water and dived. The *Alisha*'s bow rose towards him and he reached forward, searching for a handhold. The bow was wet and slimy and his hand slipped. He succeeded on his next attempt, wedging his hand in a crack on the boat's hull. Vikram clung on, battling the buoyancy that strove to float him to the surface.

A deep gash ran through the centre of the boat. A line of splintered wood traced a jagged path from the bow to the engine compartment and through to the other side. Except for the knife-like incision, the *Alisha* still looked seaworthy. But Vikram's heart was heavy as he stared at the wreck. This was to be her final resting place.

Vikram let go of the hull and surfaced. Aditya and Shaukat were floating a short distance away, near the reef. He swam towards them. Shaukat grabbed one of his hands when he arrived, Aditya held the other. The water was choppy and they had to cling to one another to prevent themselves from being swept apart.

Vikram shouted to overcome the thunder of the waves. 'Why are you so close to the reef?' he asked.

The water was turbulent and a current was pulling them towards the reef. Shaukat pointed at the seething line of froth. 'The *Alisha* hit the reef at this point,' he yelled. 'The impact tore her apart. Everything inside has spilled between the reef and where the *Alisha* is. We've recovered a few things already. Aditya is searching the area to the left, the central area is mine. You check out the water to the right. Okay?'

Vikram waved and turned away. He swam slowly, his eyes probing the sand and rocks below him. He marvelled at the clarity of the water. The previous day, the lagoon had been dark and murky. Today it was as clear as glass, the visibility underwater almost as good as that on land.

Vikram dipped low, skimming the sand. Sunlight blinked at him. He turned, searching for the source of the flash. He saw a sea anemone. In its spiky midst, he spotted a can. Kicking, he swam towards it. Two orange clownfish darted into the anemone when he approached. They stared fearfully at him as he prised the can from the anemone. Vikram worked with great care. Except for clownfish, the sea anemone stings every creature that touches it. When the can was safely in his hands, Vikram hovered above the anemone, gazing at the clownfish. The thick white stripe on their orange bodies was comical. *Maybe that was why they were called clownfish*, he thought. He was aware that clownfish are always found in sea anemones. The anemone protects them from predators and the tiny fish spend their entire lives swimming about its bush-like strands.

A short while later, Vikram spotted another can in an area heaped with shells. There were so many shells that

Vikram wondered if it was a food source that had drawn them there. It was either that or underwater currents had swept them there. Most of the shells were bivalves, but there were others too. Vikram could identify spiky spider conches and lumpy cowrie shells. The cowries were wet and slimy and alive. Here, where they lived, they bore no resemblance to the slippery smooth shells sold in shops.

Soon, the search for *Alisha*'s lost cargo slipped to the back of Vikram's mind. He spotted batfish, blue surgeons and butterfly fish. Sergeant major fish with thick black stripes floated everywhere. They were common enough here for Vikram to liken them to crows. He saw a school of large stripped fish floating beside a clump of staghorn coral. When he drew closer, he saw that they were sweetlips fish. Not far from the coral, he saw a giant clam. It was big, even larger than the one Shaukat had shown him at Kalpeni. As Vikram swam towards the clam, he startled a brown fish resting on the sand. The fish suddenly doubled in size and spines sprang from its body. A porcupine fish. Vikram hurriedly backed away. The spines that spiked out from it like thorns were poisonous.

After a length of pleasurable time, Vikram's conscience pricked him and he reverted his energies to his job. An hour later, he had found two more cans, three spoons and a frying pan. He swam to the beach and added his findings to the jumble of objects lying there.

Aditya and Shaukat had completed their search. Vikram squatted alongside them and they sorted the pile.

They had recovered a spear, a net, a first aid box, ten cans of food, five steel plates, several spoons, a knife, three drinking glasses, a packet of cooking oil, two pots and two frying pans.

Aditya looked up at the sky. 'God . . . you have been so kind,' he said with great drama. Bending, he scooped up the net from the sand. 'Look!' He shook the net, scattering sand from it. 'All these lovely fish in the water. We could only stare at them. But that's not the case any more.' He opened his mouth, flicking his tongue across his lips. 'Lunch,' he cried, waving the net vigorously. 'I can only think of lunch now.'

Vikram laughed. 'I'm with you, Aditya. Can't wait.'

Shaukat's eyes twinkled. 'You've overlooked something, haven't you?' He reached forward and retrieved the first aid box. 'We need a fire to cook the fish.'

'Oh!' said Aditya, his face falling.

Shaukat held up the first aid box. 'This is actually our most important find. The fishing net is great, but we can get along without it. It will be harder, but I can get fish with my spear.' Shaukat shook the box. 'Not only do we have medicines here, but there are also matchboxes and a cigarette lighter packed inside a watertight container. The container should hopefully have kept things dry. If it hasn't . . .' The islander shrugged. 'Then we have a problem.'

Shaukat dusted sand from the box and then carefully opened it.

Everything inside was sopping wet. Vikram held the box as Shaukat pulled out soaked cotton wool, bandages and pads. Aditya laid them to dry on palm fronds and coconut husks. In addition, there was a bottle of iodine, tubes of Betadine paste and tablets wrapped in foil.

These were intact and usable. Shaukat then plucked out a container that was wrapped in plastic. He peeled away the plastic and upturned it. A cigarette lighter and three matchboxes fell into his hand.

Shaukat flicked the knob of the lighter. Nothing happened. He tried again, but it refused to light.

'What about the matchboxes?' asked Vikram.

'They are damp,' said Shaukat. 'They won't light now.' He laughed at the boys' worried faces. 'Look at you two. Anxious, like clownfish. There's no need to worry. The matchboxes will be fine. They'll dry out in the sun. Same with the lighter. The flint inside is probably damp. A little bit of sunshine should repair it.'

Shaukat laid the matchboxes and the lighter on a dry palm frond. 'Collect as many dry fronds as you can,' he instructed the boys. 'Cut their leaves and make a pile. Meanwhile I'll get some fish for us.'

Vikram and Aditya set about their task while Shaukat entered the lagoon with the net in his hands.

He returned shortly with four pomfret-sized fish in the net.

The gas lighter worked when Shaukat flicked it. The fire burnt bright and it wasn't long before the fish were cooked and ready to eat.

The meal was delicious and consumed in silence. Afterwards, they sprawled in the shade of the palm trees and chatted. Time passed. The weather turned warm as the sun traversed the sky. They fell asleep and it was evening when they woke.

Leftover fish and baked beans were consumed as a snack.

When they were done, Shaukat turned to Aditya. 'I want you to test the windsurf board,' he said. 'Check the board out thoroughly because you're going to have to sail it to Tinakara tomorrow.'

Aditya looked questioningly at Shaukat.

'There's water on Tinakara. We've almost finished one canister. I want to fill up before Koya or the militants arrive. Tomorrow should be okay, but it could get dangerous later. So it's best you go tomorrow and stock up.'

Later, as the sun dipped in the sky, Shaukat and Vikram entered the lagoon to fish and Aditya hauled a board and a sail to the beach. Entering the water, he clipped them together and stepped on to the board.

The wind was light. It barely moved the board forward. Aditya had planned on sailing to Tinakara and back, but in these windless conditions, it wasn't possible. He decided to circle their island instead.

Aditya saw Vikram and Shaukat wave at him. He waved back. He didn't want to scare away the fish they were hunting, so he steered the board away from them, towards the reef. It was slow sailing, the board barely making headway in the light wind. Aditya pumped the sail to help move the board forward. It was tiresome. He soon grew fed up. Aditya was a boy who loved wind and speed. These conditions were no good, not fit even for beginners. A short distance from the reef, he dropped the sail and sat on the board. The water was choppy. He wasn't far from where the waves crashed against the reef. Vikram wouldn't have thought this to be a safe area, but for Aditya, it was fine.

Aditya decided on a swim. There was plenty of coral here and he wanted to explore. Slipping off the board, he entered the water. Coral blossomed everywhere about him, the organisms packed tight, like trees in a rainforest. Every colour he could think of was splashed before him and the shapes and symmetries were bizarre, like the imaginations of a crazed artist. After feasting on the coral with his eyes, Aditya decided to look out at the sea. For this, he would have to stand on the coral. The only flat surface was a tabletop coral nearby. He would have to be careful though because it was surrounded by the hard and spiny stalks of staghorn coral. He swam to the table-shaped coral and placed his feet on it. It felt sturdy under him. He stood up shakily, half his body out of the water.

It was pleasant standing there. He could see the dark waters of the open sea stretching away to the horizon. He watched the waves froth as they broke against the reef. Their fine spray caught the sunlight and broke it into shimmering rainbows.

From the corner of his eye, he saw the windsurf board drifting towards the reef. Aditya stepped forward, unmindful of the sharp coral tentacles surrounding him and cried out in pain. A burning sensation shot through his right foot. His impulsive stride had raked his foot against the sharp spines of the staghorn coral. He lost balance as he doubled over, clutching his foot.

A dark red stain coloured the water.

Aditya knew he was badly hurt. He was bleeding profusely. 'Sharks!' was his first thought. His earlier encounter with them was fresh in his mind. He had to get to the board. He swam fast, shutting out his pain. The board had drifted a considerable distance. He prayed there were no sharks about. He was spewing a trail of blood.

Aditya cried out in relief on reaching the board. He dragged himself on to it and placed both his feet on it. Blood pumped from his right foot, colouring the board red. There was no time to waste; he had to head for the shore. He pulled himself upright and balancing on one foot, he tugged at the sail. The water was turbulent. The board wobbled dangerously as the sail emerged from the water. It pitched and rocked violently. With two good feet, Aditya would have easily handled the board, but lame and single-footed, it was impossible, and he tumbled clumsily into the water.

He clambered back, fearful of sharks. His foot hurt terribly and blood continued to gush from it. The board was drifting ever closer to the reef. He had to act quickly, otherwise he would soon be cast on the reef, at the mercy of its waves. He turned his head, looking for Shaukat and Vikram. He saw them in the distance. They were done with their fishing and were wading back to the shore, their backs turned to him.

'Vikram . . . Shaukat . . . HELP!' yelled Aditya. There was no response, they continued their walk towards the beach.

'HELP!' he shouted again. But it was no use; they could not hear him. His voice was being drowned by the roar of the waves. He could shout himself hoarse and they would never hear him.

Waves thundered about him. Aditya was no match for such monstrous waves, especially with an injured foot. He would be swept like driftwood and crushed against the reef. He had to make a decision soon. Should he abandon the board and swim to the shore, trailing blood and inviting the possibility of a shark attack; or should he attempt sailing the board despite his injured foot?

Aditya decided to stay with the board.

But he would have to move fast as the board was being sucked towards the reef. Aditya dragged himself to an upright position, carefully balancing on one leg. He reached for the uphaul rope. The board lurched as a wave slapped it. Aditya fell, sprawling on to the sail. The coral surface was less than two feet under him. He was almost on the reef. A frothing wave, moving like an express train, roared into the reef. The spray showered Aditya and stung his eyes. It rocked the board, threatening to drag it away from Aditya's clutching hands.

Aditya sprang back on to the board, disregarding the pain in his leg. This was his last chance. If he fell now, he would surely be cast on to the reef. He grabbed the uphaul line, using it to balance himself. He carefully pulled the sail. It swung free of the water.

This was a crucial moment. He had to transfer his hands to the boom and power the sail. Under normal circumstances, Aditya could do this with his eyes closed, but on one leg and in a frothing sea, it was different. Aditya hesitated. He hung on, unable to summon the courage to commit himself. Another wave tore into the reef, surging over his board, submerging his legs to his knees. Aditya wobbled dangerously on the board. It was now or never.

Moving smoothly, he transferred his grip from the mast to the boom and pulled the sail. The board lurched forward as the wind filled the sail, powering it forward.

'That's it!' he exulted. The board slowly gathered speed. It rode the choppy waters, sailing away from the reef. Just one minute . . . All he needed was one minute, and he would be out of danger.

A wave caught the board from starboard, swinging it viciously. The sail momentarily lost the wind. It started to fall backwards on to Aditya. He felt himself losing balance. Aditya brought his injured leg down, mercilessly transferring his weight on to it. The pain was staggering, but Aditya fought it, clawing his foot to the board. Tears welled in his eyes. His leg felt as if it was dipped in a pot of molten metal.

The board gathered speed. The water grew calmer as he coasted along. Aditya knew the worst was over. Soon he felt safe enough to raise his injured foot and balance on one leg. His foot throbbed intensely.

Aditya did not remember much of the remaining journey to the shore. Fighting his pain and the sea, he guided the board back. He collapsed in a heap as the board touched the shore.

TURTLE

V ikram and Shaukat saw the board come in from the reef.
'The windsurf is doing fine,' said Vikram, shielding
his eyes against the setting sun.

The sail wobbled and the board moved sluggishly
across the water.

'Not much of a wind. Is that why he's going so slow?'
asked Vikram.

'He's sailing badly,' said Shaukat. He looked closely.
'Could something be wrong with the board?'

They watched the board as it touched down and then
looked on in alarm when Aditya collapsed. They dropped
the fish they were holding and ran towards him.

Aditya grunted and cried in pain as his friends dragged
him ashore. They eased him to a sitting position and
examined his leg. The injured portion was red and raw.
Vikram rushed off and returned with the medical box
and water in a glass. Vikram helped Aditya sip water and
Shaukat cleaned his wound.

It was a nasty injury. Three deep gashes split the heel
of Aditya's foot. Shaukat washed them with seawater.

He then disinfected the wound with antiseptic paste. The bleeding continued for some time. When it stopped, he applied more paste and wrapped a bandage around it.

Darkness had set in by the time they finished with Aditya. He was thoroughly exhausted and they left him to rest. Vikram and Shaukat built a fire from palm fronds and busied themselves cooking a dinner of fresh fish.

After dinner, they sat on the beach watching a pale sickle moon fall to the sea. Aditya slept beside them. The gentlest of breezes blew in from the sea. The lagoon was silent. Not a wave, not a murmur. Just the odd flash of phosphorescence where its water lapped the shore.

Shaukat stared out across the lagoon. 'Aditya behaved stupidly,' he said. 'I've heard about your diving trip at Kadmat where he was irresponsible too. Is he always like this?'

Vikram sighed. 'What can I say? It's not that he deliberately chases trouble. That's not how it is. To understand Aditya, you have to know him. He has a tremendous sense of self-belief. He is strong. He is an athlete. He is a great sailor. He's one of the best swimmers in school. As you can expect, this goes to his head. Makes him super confident. That's where a sense of invincibility creeps in. His confidence bubbles over and gets him into trouble.'

Shaukat sifted sand through his fingers. 'Confidence is all very well. But there is a line between boldness and stupidity. Aditya was lucky today. Lagoons are deceptive. Mostly, there is no danger. But for a foolish person or a tough guy like Aditya, danger lurks everywhere.

'For all its serenity, the lagoon is not a swimming pool. It is alive. It is home to thousands of creatures. Most are harmless, but some aren't. For us, the lagoons are an extension of our island. They are our home. For you mainlanders, the cities are your home. Just as you are careful about crossing the road, we are mindful in our lagoons. I would never have dreamt of windsurfing in the area Aditya chose to go to today.'

The sickle moon set in the far horizon, robbing the sea of its shimmer. The beach sloped from where they sat to the water. The sand bordering the water was alive with creatures. Vikram squinted in the darkness. It seemed as if the creatures were shells. They travelled in short bursts across the sand, halting and then shooting off again. Vikram could see claws and tentacles being extended and retracted from under the shells.

'What are they?' queried Vikram.

'Hermit crabs,' replied Shaukat.

Vikram stared. 'They look a bit strange for crabs . . . as if their shells don't fit them.'

'That's right. Their shells don't fit them.' Shaukat laughed. 'Hermits aren't your regular crabs. They don't have an armoured bony structure. Most crabs have a hard protective covering. But hermits—even though they are crabs—do not. They are defenceless. Their soft unprotected abdomens are easy targets for predators who can rip them open. So hermits search desperately for something to shield their bodies with. They take whatever they can find. Mostly they pick up discarded shells.

133

But they even take stuff like bottle caps.' Shaukat laughed again. 'They can look really funny.'

Vikram stared at the waterline. There was a hermit party happening there. Crabs in large numbers were proudly parading the shells they had found. All shapes and all sizes were on display: some as small as bottle caps, others as large as cowrie shells.

The two friends chatted idly. Vikram was surprised to learn that Shaukat had never set foot on the mainland till he was fifteen years old.

Shaukat smiled as he recollected his first visit. 'It was a terrible experience. I had never seen a city. I wasn't prepared for the people, or the crowds, or the roads and the traffic. I couldn't cross the road; what with rickshaws hurtling about and buses roaring past. I had never felt so scared in all my life. The sea is a much safer place.'

Vikram held back a smile.

'Cyclists kept bumping into me. They were rude and called me names. Nobody had time for anybody. Here it so different. We are a gentle and trusting people. We leave our houses open and nobody steals. There are no robberies. Sometimes I wish we weren't so trusting. People make fools of those who trust. My father had warned me to be careful of my bag on the mainland. I didn't believe him and I learnt my lesson quickly. On the first day, my wallet was robbed, on the second, my suitcase disappeared. It was terrible. I wanted to return to my islands. But my father made me stay. One day, he took me to the mountains. I was fascinated; I never thought that the land could grow so tall. There were so many different trees. There were fields, rivers and forests. It was all so beautiful. You mainlanders take these things for granted, but we islanders do not get to see these things. Our islands are flat, no mountains, no rivers, no forests, no animals, not even dogs. I hate the cities of the mainland. But the mountains, the forests, the valleys are very beautiful.'

'Would you prefer to live on the mainland?'

Shaukat laughed. 'Never. Ask any islander. All will say no. Our islands are a part of us. You can never separate them from our souls.'

Vikram and Shaukat talked about the islands, the stars and the seas. Time held no meaning for them. They were no pressing tasks for the morning. The sun would rise, they would fish and cook and drink coconut water.

A crisp night breeze blew across the island. It was warm and bore the smell of salt. As Vikram gazed at the water, he saw something dark emerge from it. It paused at the water's edge. It was big and rounded, like an upturned bowl on the sloping sand. Vikram instantly knew what it was. He clutched Shaukat's hand and hissed: 'Turtle!'

They both stared at the armoured creature. It remained still for a long while, water sloshing about it. When it finally moved, its flippers emerged, displacing sand instead of water. The turtle huffed itself to dry sand and halted again.

'It's hard work for the animal,' Shaukat spoke in a whisper.

Sea turtles are heavy creatures. In the sea, they are weightless. But when they emerge from the water, their bulkiness burdens them, pressing them deep into the sand.

Vikram's heart was beating rapidly. Turtles were high on his father's list of favourite animals. Vikram had learnt about them from him. He knew that they lived their entire lives in the sea. He also knew that although they were marine animals, they had a connection to land, a deep, umbilical connection. A connection that has persisted through the ages. Sea turtles don't lay their eggs in the sea. They lay them on land. This turtle was a female. She had come to the island to lay her eggs.

They woke Aditya and the three of them watched as the turtle agonizingly heaved herself up the beach. The animal seemed hopelessly out of place on land. Vikram was reminded of walruses as he gazed at the turtle. Walruses too are clumsy on land, and like turtles, they are fluid and graceful in the sea.

'Should we help it?' asked Aditya.

'No,' replied Vikram and Shaukat together.

The turtle dragged herself past a palm tree and halted.

'She will dig soon,' said Shaukat. 'She has passed the high-tide line.'

Vikram explained for Aditya. 'The eggs aren't safe below the tideline. The sea will sweep them away. So they dig their nest hole only when they are beyond the tide's reach.'

The turtle lumbered about and selected a sandy area. She settled herself and started sweeping sand with her flippers.

Vikram's father was deeply concerned about sea turtles. Their numbers were decreasing worldwide, he had said.

Every day hundreds die in fishing nets. But it wasn't those losses alone that were endangering them. The biggest threat to their survival is their ancestral connection to land. Earlier, this wasn't a problem. The tropical coastlines of Earth were largely free of humans. But that wasn't the case any more. Humans now occupy most of the sandy beaches on this planet. We disrupt their life cycle. We raid their nests and steal their eggs. We kill them for their meat, or for their shells, or sometimes just for the fun of it.

The turtle shovelled sand with her flippers. She created a depression in the sand, which quickly deepened into a hole. The hole would soon be suitable for her eggs. During egg laying, turtles turn oblivious to their surroundings.

Vikram waited for a while. Then he called his friends forward. 'Come,' he said. 'She's probably laying her eggs now.'

They walked quietly to the turtle. She sat in her hole, looking every bit a prehistoric creature. Eggs, the size of golf balls, were oozing stickily from her rear end. The turtle cocked her reptilian head at them. She inspected them and then looked away.

The boys counted the eggs as they fell. They applauded when the hundredth one plopped into the pile. The count was nearing 150 by the time the turtle was done. She rose and shovelled sand again. The boys helped, shifting chunks of sand with their hands. The pit filled quickly and soon it was entirely covered.

Inside lay a stockpile of precious eggs, each with its own baby turtle. The mother turtle's work was done. She would soon return to the sea. The eggs would lie there, incubating in the sand. They would crack open some sixty days later and baby turtles would dig their way out of the egg chamber. Once on the surface, they would make a run for the sea. But predators lie in wait. Crabs grab the helpless creatures in their claws and birds scoop them up in their beaks. Many hatchlings perish on this run. For those that make it to the sea, it is only the beginning of a grim struggle for survival. It is said that from a clutch of 100 eggs, barely a handful make it to adulthood. This is why female turtles lay so many eggs. Their prolific bounty ensures the survival of the species.

Turtles weren't the best of mothers, thought Vikram as they escorted the reptile to the beach. This individual had laid her eggs, and as per the norms of her species, her job was done. The fate of her offspring was not her concern. She was abandoning them. They were on their own.

The turtle stopped often on its journey back to the sea. Land was clearly not the animal's habitat. She was utterly helpless here. *It was the easiest thing to flip her on her back*, thought Vikram. They could kill her and feast on turtle meat. But he would never do that and he was sure that such a thought would not occur to his friends either.

The turtle pressed deep tracks into the sand. *Like a truck*, thought Vikram as he followed it. When it finally reached the water, it halted. It turned its head and looked at the boys. Then it floated out into the lagoon. The turtle quickly gathered speed, gliding through the water. They tracked it till it suddenly submerged itself, disappearing into the dark depths of the sea.

TRAPPED

The next morning was bright and sunny. Vikram and Shaukat woke early and went fishing. Aditya slept long and late, waking only when breakfast was cooked and ready.

'How's the leg?' queried Vikram.

Aditya inspected his bandaged foot. Then he looked at Vikram and shook his head.

'We'll change the dressing,' said Vikram, 'Sorry, but you will have to rest today.'

'And no swimming or windsurfing,' said Shaukat.

Aditya made a face but did not protest.

After the wound was dressed, the boys discussed plans for the day.

'I'm going to build us a shelter,' said Shaukat.

He turned to Vikram. 'You will have to take on Aditya's job and sail to Tinakara to fetch water. There's no sign of the militants yet, but they could turn up any time. It's best you leave soon. Take the empty can with you and both the windsurf boards.'

Vikram raised his eyebrows. 'Both boards?'

'You will need two boards,' said Shaukat. 'How do you expect to bring the jerrycan back? Getting to Tinakara won't be a problem. The can is empty and will float behind you. But when you fill it with water, it will turn heavy and sink. You won't be able to tow it back.'

'I get it,' said Aditya. 'We strap the jerrycan to the extra board and Vikram will tow the board behind him.'

Shaukat nodded. 'Come on,' he said. 'Let's rig the boards together.'

They worked quickly, tying the boards to one another. They strapped the can to the trailing board and fixed the sail to the lead one.

When they were done, Vikram tugged the boards into the water. Shaukat and Aditya bid goodbye to him.

'You've got to help us build the shelter,' called out Aditya as Vikram stepped on to the board. 'No goofing off and hanging about the island. Come back soon'.

Vikram laughed as he pulled up the sail. He waved at them as the board gathered speed.

'Safe journey,' shouted Shaukat.

Vikram's heart lifted as the boards splashed forward. It felt good to be sailing again.

Ahead, Tinakara Island was clearly visible. The island lay flat and low, like a long cigar on the far horizon.

The wind was ideal. Not too strong yet not too mild—it filled the sail and sped him along at a pleasurable pace. The water was turquoise and sparklingly transparent. Clumps of coral flashed past beneath him. Seagrass swirled in underwater currents. Turtles foraged in the grass and brightly coloured fish darted beneath the board.

Pitti Island shrank behind him and Tinakara expanded. At some point, it struck Vikram that he was alone. Just him and his windsurf board in a vast expanse of water. He should have felt lonely. Perhaps even worried. But Vikram felt neither. A great happiness suffused him instead. The lagoon was breathtakingly beautiful—a turquoise jewel that dazzled with its light. The wind was perfect and the sun was bright and warm. What more could he have asked for?

Time passed and Tinakara drew close. The island was very long—many times the size of Pitti. Palm trees fluttered in the wind and a white beach blinked in the sunlight. Even from a distance, evidence of the departed storm was visible. Fallen palm trees lay everywhere and the beach was strewn with seagrass and broken fronds. An acute sense of loneliness radiated from the island. Vikram could feel it. The fallen trees and the storm-littered beach added to the desolation. So did the empty sky and sea. There were no birds, no lizards, no sign of life. It was as if the world had abandoned Tinakara.

Vikram touched down on a long curving beach.

Shaukat had said that there were two wells on the island. One wasn't far from where he had landed. His instructions were to walk west along the beach, which Vikram did, and in minutes he came upon it.

The well was a square hole in the ground. It was filled with clear, clean water and there were steps that led into it.

141

Deepak Dalal

Vikram descended the steps and drank. The water was everything he wanted it to be: sweet, cool and refreshing. When he was done, he filled the jerrycan. The source of the water in the well wasn't rainwater. Rain added to the well water, no doubt. But the real source, the perennial one, was the sea itself. The sand on the island was a natural filter that strained the seawater. It removed the salt and sweetened it, and the resulting water (fit to drink) bubbled to the surface at the well.

Vikram hauled the jerrycan back to the boards. He would have to head back soon, but Shaukat had permitted him a quick exploration of the island. Shading his eyes, he examined the beach. It was long and it curved into the distance, terminating beneath an elevated mound of land. The mound was the highest point of the island. Shaukat had recommended climbing it. The entire island was visible from there, he had said, including a sheltered bay on the far side, where visitors moored their boats.

Vikram strolled along the beach. It was warm and still and silent. On the sand, he finally saw signs of life—crabs and a lone sandpiper bird. The sandpiper accompanied Vikram on his walk. When he drew near, it would fly and settle a short distance ahead. When he came close again, it would take off and touch down further along the beach. In this manner, Vikram soon reached the mound. He sweated as he climbed it. At the top, he looked down at the other side of the island.

A long stretch of beach glowed dully in the sunlight. At its far end, the beach arched in the shape of a bow.

Inside the bow was an area of deep, calm water. Shaukat was right. Tinakara had a perfect bay for parking boats; infinitely better than anything Pitti could offer.

Vikram looked out across the reef, to the sea. In the distance, he saw two boats. Their dark outlines stood out sharply against the blue of the sea. At first, Vikram did not register their presence. They fitted so well with the lagoon and the beach that it seemed only natural that they be there.

Then, like a tsunami, the implication of their presence struck him.

'Boats!' Vikram's heart soared. 'Boats! We are saved.' He thrust his hands skyward and whooped with joy. Then he froze, his hands still above his head. His euphoria vanished and the breath exited his lungs. *What if they were Basheer Koya's boats?*

Vikram suddenly felt exposed on the mound. He ducked swiftly behind a tree.

Vikram struggled to control his racing heart. If they were Basheer Koya's boats, he was done for. He looked back at Pitti Island. It was too far. The boats would enter the lagoon before he was even halfway there. They would see him and chase him down. Vikram prayed that the boats were friendly.

Vikram flattened himself on the mud. A fallen palm lay nearby. Crawling forward, he hid behind it.

The boats weren't the regular island fishing vessels. They were bigger. Their lines were sleeker, intended for travel and leisure. It wasn't long before the first boat arrived at the reef entrance. He heard the beat of its engine.

The pilot dropped his speed, edging forward, avoiding the coral lurking beneath. Soon, both boats had entered the lagoon. They motored towards the deep water of the bay.

Several men crowded the deck of the boats. They wore T-shirts and lungis. One individual stood separately on the prow of the leading vessel, waving his arms and issuing instructions to the boat pilot. He was short and fat, and he wore a wide panama hat.

Vikram's breath caught in his throat. 'Oh no,' he breathed.

He was trapped. The fat man was none other than the dreaded Basheer Koya.

The first boat cut its engine. Two men jumped into the water and swam to the beach.

The sight of the men jolted Vikram. They would soon be swarming all over the island. The mound was exposed, the wrong place to be. He had to hide.

Crouching, Vikram descended the mound. Straightening, he readied to run to the beach, and halted.

Footprints! He would leave footprints on the sand.

But what about his earlier prints? He had walked extensively on the beach. His footprints were already imprinted on the sand.

Vikram ran. There was nothing he could do about the footprints. He could only hope. The island was big. The men might not cross to this side.

Vikram arrived breathlessly beside the boards. He dismantled the one he had used and wrapped the sail around the mast. There was an area nearby where several palm trees had come down together. He dragged both the boards, the mast and the jerrycan there and tucked them beneath the fallen palm fronds. Then he swept the area, erasing drag marks and his footprints.

Vikram inspected his work. The boards and the jerrycan were well hidden. Unless someone ventured into the area they wouldn't be found. He squeezed himself under the palm fronds and lay down on a board.

Time passed. His breathing eased. His head cleared. He started to think clearly. He couldn't return to Pitti Island. Not during the day at least. His sail was too conspicuous. He would be spotted instantly. He would have to wait till it was dark. He could sail back then.

Faisal!

Vikram controlled a sudden urge to sit up. Faisal must be here on Tinakara Island. Basheer Koya would surely have brought the boy with him. It was far too risky for him to have left Faisal behind on Kalpeni.

Faisal's presence changed everything. He could no longer just wait for dark and sail back to Pitti.

Since the shipwreck and their subsequent marooning on Pitti Island, Vikram, Aditya and Shaukat had spoken only once about Faisal. They had discussed his fate, studying it from every angle, and the heart-wrenching conclusion they had come to had hurt them so much that they hadn't talked about Faisal again.

Their reasoning was simple. Besides his accomplices, only four others were aware of Basheer Koya's complicity in Kumar's kidnapping. Of these, Basheer Koya believed that three of them—Shaukat, Vikram and Aditya—were dead, killed in the storm. That left only Faisal. Basheer Koya was a ruthless man. It didn't require a high degree of intelligence to guess Faisal's fate.

But Vikram's thinking differed from his friends'. Vikram was the kind of boy who had faith in the innate goodness of humankind. Basheer Koya might be a thief, a murderer, a kidnapper, but Faisal was his nephew. The man had to have a conscience. He might be forced to kill his nephew eventually. But he wouldn't perform the grisly act straightaway. He would postpone it for as long as he could. In Vikram's opinion, Faisal was alive and on one of the boats. If that were the case—and Vikram was certain it was so—then escape to Pitti was no longer his goal. He had to find Faisal first and then engineer his escape.

Vikram slipped into deep thought.

Basheer Koya and his men had come here to meet the militants. Kumar was to be handed over to them here, on Tinakara Island. Faisal had told them so. Vikram did not know when the militants would come. They could arrive today, or at the latest, tomorrow. That didn't leave him much time. If he managed to plot a rescue plan, it would have to be executed this very night.

It wasn't safe to search for Faisal now. Basheer Koya's men would be docking the boats and setting up camp. Vikram would have to wait till things were more settled, when the men were resting.

Vikram immersed himself in thought. He considered different possibilities, examining each one in detail.

He deliberated on the boats, of what use they might be to him. He speculated on Shaukat and Aditya, mulling ways of involving them in the rescue attempt.

Time passed. It was hot under the trees. Insects bothered Vikram. The air was still. Soon drowsiness overcame him and he fell asleep.

When he woke, it was afternoon. The sun had crossed its zenith and shadows were lengthening.

Vikram rose. The silence around him was absolute. The trees stood mute; no wind rustling them. Even the sea was quiet; its murmuring so faint that he couldn't hear it. The area was deserted. Basheer Koya's men hadn't visited.

To get to the bay where the boats were parked, Vikram would have to cut through the trees to the other side of the island. This wasn't going to be easy. The foliage on Tinakara was thick and overgrown. Breaking through it would be hard work. Yet Vikram was thankful for the trees. They provided excellent cover, permitting him to sneak in close without being detected.

Vikram sweated as he made his way through the trees. The conditions were like a steam bath, hot and sticky. But more than the oven-like heat, what troubled him was the mess of palm fronds on the ground. He had to pick his way through the clutter and yet ensure that his passage was quiet.

The sparkle of water through the trees warned him that the beach was near. He dropped on all fours and crawled the final distance to the boundary where the trees yielded to sand and the sea. Selecting a tree that arched elegantly across the beach, he tucked himself behind it. Keeping low, he edged his head across its trunk.

The first thing Vikram spotted were the boats. They bobbed quietly in the turquoise waters of the bay.

The empty decks indicated that there was no one aboard the boats. Closer, on the beach, two large tents were pitched. Several men lay sprawled on the sand outside the tents. Some were asleep, others were chatting or playing cards. A motorized rubber dinghy floated in the water beside the men.

There was no sign of Faisal.

Could Faisal be in the tents? Even Basheer Koya wasn't visible. He and Faisal could both be resting inside the tents. Vikram counted the men on the sand. There were twelve. He scrutinized each of the men and he tensed when he saw that one had a gun strapped to his back. The gunman was bearded and well built. He was playing cards and his laughter and swearing carried across the beach to Vikram.

The tents were a sign that Basheer Koya and his men planned to spend time on the island. They had arrived early and were waiting for the militants to turn up.

Vikram grew worried as time passed without sign of Faisal. Could he have been wrong? Could Faisal have been left behind at Kalpeni? Or . . . Vikram brushed away the thought that came to him. Instead, he convinced himself that Faisal was in the tents, sheltering from the sun. Vikram's guess was accurate because a short while later, a short boy with a bushy mop of hair emerged from one of the tents.

Faisal!

Vikram controlled an impulse to punch the air. His friend was alive and well. A rush of happiness warmed his chest.

Vikram watched as Faisal stretched. He saw him blink, adjusting his eyes to the glare of the sun. Then he started walking. Vikram's breath quickened. Faisal was walking in his direction.

Faisal strode past the men on the sand. The well-built man with the gun called out. Faisal ignored him and kept walking. One of the men on the sand rose and ran to Faisal, blocking his path. Faisal turned and shouted angrily at the man with the gun. The gunman reached into his pockets. He extracted something and tossed it to the friend who barred Faisal's path. The object gleamed metallically in the sunlight as the man caught it. He grabbed Faisal's hands and performed some quick juggling with the shiny object and then walked away. Faisal shouted angrily at the men. They responded by laughing uproariously. Faisal turned away and, in a temper, continued on his interrupted journey.

Vikram could see that the glittering object was a pair of handcuffs. Basheer Koya's men were not taking any chances. Vikram chuckled. Faisal must have inflicted serious trouble on his captors for them to shackle his hands on a remote island like Tinakara where there wasn't much scope for mischief.

Faisal walked forward.

Vikram's heart beat faster. He prayed that Faisal would keep coming. But the islander's pace slackened and he

149

turned to the water. He wet his feet and kicked at the sand. After a while, he crossed to the palm trees bordering the shore and settled himself not far from Vikram. Leaning against a tree, Faisal whistled softly to himself.

Vikram had to draw Faisal's attention. He searched the sand for something to throw at him. Several walnut-sized baby coconuts lay in the sand. Vikram gathered them and selected one. He glanced at Basheer Koya's men. They were caught up in their gossip and laughter. Vikram gently lobbed the coconut at Faisal. It landed in the sand near Faisal's feet. Faisal continued to hum, undisturbed by the coconut.

Vikram threw another coconut, this time with more force, aiming directly at Faisal. It hit Faisal on his shoulder and bounced away. Faisal stopped humming. He sat up and stared. Vikram raised his head, allowing Faisal to catch a glimpse of him, and dropped back to the sand.

Faisal's eyes almost popped out of their sockets. Vikram! That face, which had appeared for only an instant, was Vikram's. But Vikram, Aditya and Shaukat were dead. They had gone out on the day of that dreadful storm and had never come back. The navy had searched for them, but neither they nor their boat had been found.

Vikram stifled his laughter as Faisal's chin started to tremble. His face had turned pale, like he had seen a ghost.

Vikram threw again and hit Faisal on his chin. Repeating the earlier sequence, he lifted his head and ducked.

This time, Faisal glared. Ghost or no ghost, that coconut had hurt.

Vikram poked his head out once more, waving and retreating behind his tree.

Faisal breathed deeply. He glanced at his captors. They were paying no attention to him. He sat up clumsily, his hands still locked together. He walked to Vikram's tree and collapsed on the sand.

His lips moved. He tried to speak but what emerged from him could best be described as a kind of croaking noise.

Vikram had no such trouble. 'Hi Faisal,' he greeted cheerily.

Faisal's lips stirred again, but like before, all Vikram heard were frog-like croaks.

Vikram laughed. 'No, I'm not a ghost, Faisal. I'm alive. All three of us are alive. Aditya, Shaukat and I survived the storm.' Vikram briefly narrated their sea adventure and shipwreck.

'You frightened me,' said Faisal, finally finding his voice. 'Gave me a heart attack. I was certain that you were dead. I cried so much. The storm was terrible. It brought down half the trees on Kalpeni. My uncle told me that all of you were dead and I believed him. Then, I see your head pop up and disappear. You can imagine my fright! Don't you ever do that again. You'll kill someone next time.'

Vikram laughed silently.

'Enjoy yourself,' muttered Faisal.

Vikram reigned in his amusement. 'Why did they put handcuffs on you?' he asked.

Faisal made a sound somewhere between a snort and a laugh. 'They don't trust me. I emptied a can of petrol on the foredeck and tried to light it after we left Kalpeni. Since then, they handcuff me most of the time.'

Vikram cheered Faisal's sabotage effort with a loud 'Shabash!' Then he inquired about Kumar.

Faisal sighed. 'He's in the tent with me. Poor fellow, he can't move. He has handcuffs on his hands and feet, and they never let him out of their sight. The militants are arriving tomorrow. I heard my uncle talking to them on the radio. They will hand over the ransom money and take Kumar with them. I feel sorry for him. He is miserable. I haven't had much of a chance to talk to him. He's been locked in the hold of the boat all this while. I met him for the first time today when they put us together in the tent.'

Vikram absorbed the information. 'What are they going to do with you, Faisal?' he asked. 'Kumar will be handed over tomorrow and your uncle's mission will be complete. What plans do they have for you?'

There was a silence before Faisal replied. 'I don't know,' he said in a small voice.

Vikram spoke briskly. 'Listen, Faisal. We're not going to abandon you. I have a plan. I was hoping for more time, but the militants will be here tomorrow, so we're going to have to act tonight.'

'Thanks, Vikram. I know you and the others are worried about me. I'm blessed to have friends like you.' Faisal paused, his voice quivering. 'But let's be realistic. These men are hardened criminals. They have guns and they outnumber us. There's no way you can rescue me. If you try, you'll be captured and will suffer my fate. Forget about any rescue. You are safe on Pitti. Nobody will discover you there. Save yourselves. I will look after myself.'

Vikram spoke sharply. 'Don't be an idiot, Faisal. Your uncle is not going to let you go. You know far too much. Nephew or not, he will get rid of you. So listen to me. I have a plan. If we get it right, we can defeat your uncle. We can win this. Win it together.'

Vikram quizzed Faisal before explaining his plan.

'How many guns do they have?' he asked.

'Two machine guns,' replied Faisal. 'One with Krishnan, the guy with the gun, and the other with my uncle. Some of the men have small firearms.'

'Do the boats have a radio?' questioned Vikram.

'Yes, the bigger one does.'

Vikram breathed a sigh of relief. The radio was vital to his plan.

'Does anybody sleep on the boats?'

Faisal thought for a while. 'I'm not sure,' he replied. 'But I would guess that at least one of the captains will spend the night on board.'

Vikram explained his plan to Faisal. The islander was sceptical at first, but hope kindled in him as Vikram revealed the details. It was a bold plan. A plan born out of desperation. A plan so audacious that it might actually work.

'I must leave now,' said Vikram when he was done. 'You've been sitting here long enough. I don't want them coming here to see what's up. There's too much at stake. Be prepared tonight. It's our one and only chance. We have to make it work.'

'It will work,' said Faisal. 'Goodbye, Vikram. Take care. Don't be in a hurry to return to Pitti. Wait until it's completely dark.'

Vikram bid Faisal goodbye and crawled into the underbrush.

Hampered by his handcuffs, Faisal rose with difficulty. Then he walked to the tents.

BLIND VOYAGE

Vikram retreated to his hiding place and lay down on the board once more. Pangs of hunger troubled him. Ignoring them, he absorbed himself with his plans for the night. Vikram was a methodical boy. He deliberated on every aspect of the mission. He speculated probabilities. He analysed his responses. He considered unforeseen outcomes and he constantly reviewed and fine-tuned his plans.

Late in the evening, he was disturbed by the roar of a motorboat engine. He guessed that it was Basheer Koya's men taking a spin around the island in the motorized dinghy he had seen earlier. Vikram suddenly tensed. Would they motor their dinghy to Pitti? If they did so, Aditya and Shaukat would surely be discovered. But the sound of the motor remained constant. Vikram relaxed. The men were taking a joyride around Tinakara.

Soon darkness fell. A sickle moon shed its pale light on the island. Vikram wasn't willing to chance sailing in moonlight. If someone was watching, they might see him. In any case, at this stage of its cycle, the moon set early. He wouldn't have to wait long.

Later, as the moon fell to the horizon, Vikram dragged one board and the sail to the shore. The jerrycan was heavy and so, he had decided to abandon it along with the extra board. Working quickly, he rigged the sail and attached the mast to the board.

Vikram waited.

A strong breeze was blowing across the island, rustling the palms overhead. The wind brought cheer to Vikram. His return to Pitti would be swift if it continued to blow like this. The moon sank into the sea and the sky turned dark.

It was time.

Vikram dragged his board into the water and mounted it. When he lifted the sail, the wind filled it and powered the board forward. Dark water washed over his legs as the board picked up speed.

As he drew away from Tinakara, Vikram noticed a flickering light at the far end of the island. Basheer Koya and his men had lit a fire. Vikram's eyes were drawn to the fire, and as he stared, it struck him how useful its light would be. The fire would provide a fix on Tinakara's location. Like a compass, it would provide a bearing throughout the voyage.

Except for the fire, there was darkness everywhere. The sky bristled with stars. But the countless pinpricks of light were hopelessly inadequate to illumine the gloom of the night. It was so dark that Vikram couldn't even see the horizon. It was as if the sea had swallowed the sky. Vikram couldn't tell one from the other.

Fear clutched at Vikram's heart. There was no sign of Pitti Island, not even a shadow. How was he to set course to Pitti if he couldn't see it? The island was a speck in the vastness of the lagoon. In the darkness, he would sail past it. Even if by luck he drew near the island, he still might not see it. He would sail on and crash into the reef instead. A shiver of fear ran through Vikram as he remembered the choppy waters of the reef and the jagged wall of coral it housed.

Vikram cast his thoughts back to the morning voyage, recalling the lay of the islands. His best hope was to sail a course reverse to the one he had sailed earlier. For most of the journey to Tinakara, he had steered to starboard. Now, on the return, to retrace his voyage, he would have to sail to starboard again. Vikram pulled the sail, altering his direction, until the glow of Basheer Koya's fire lay to the left behind him. His navigation mechanism was crude. Yes, Pitti Island did lie in this direction. But his bearing was a general one. General directions worked fine when they were backed with visual inputs. Unfortunately, the night masked visual aids. For all purposes, he was sailing blind. There was little he could do except hope and pray.

Vikram sailed on. The morning voyage could not have been more starkly different. It had been bright then, and warm, and the lagoon had shone with light. On this leg, it was as if someone had hit a switch and the light had vanished, stranding him in a world of darkness. The joy, the fun, the enjoyment were gone. He was tense and fearful instead.

Even the occurrence of phosphorescence on the lagoon did little to quiet Vikram's anxiety. Everywhere around him splotches of green light clicked on and off in the water like tiny bulbs. Behind him, his board trailed a green wake too. But tonight, this spectacle of the ocean held no delight for him.

There was a sudden splashing sound and Vikram saw a flash of green shoot under his board. Vikram's chest tightened. What could it be? A shark? Vikram's hands started to shake. The sail lost power and the board wobbled dangerously. A gust of wind caught the sail, tearing it from Vikram's hands. Vikram lunged for the sail, but he was too late. His momentum unbalanced him and he cried out in terror as he tumbled head first into the water.

Vikram panicked as every trace of light disappeared. An impenetrable blackness closed in about him. He flailed his arms, reaching for the surface. Something sharp brushed his leg. Vikram kicked out in terror. His leg swung unhindered through the water, pulling him under. Something, possibly the same creature, struck his back, streaking painfully across it. Vikram writhed in fear and pain. What was it? Where was it? Terror gripped him. Vikram thrashed about, losing control of himself. His head broke clear of the water. Not pausing to breathe, he swam as fast as he could, racing away from whatever it was that had struck him. He swam far, halting only when he could go no further.

Vikram paddled his legs, keeping himself afloat. He panted, sucking deep breaths of air.

Where was the board?

He pumped his legs, trying to rise above the water. A gentle swell rode the sea. The swell hadn't troubled him on the board, but in the water, it limited his vision. He turned in circles, desperately seeking the board. It was no use. All he saw was water. Dark, black water.

A crushing sense of loss overcame him. He had lost the board. He had lost his means of transport to Pitti. Without it, he couldn't get to the island; he could not swim so far in the dark. A wave of bitterness swept over him. How could he have been so irresponsible? How could he have messed up so? The loss of the board was a calamity. A calamity with far-reaching consequences. Faisal and Kumar were doomed. All his planning would come to naught. And it was all his fault.

Suddenly a whiplash-like sound came hard and fast towards him. Vikram flung himself to the side. What was that? A flying fish, a barracuda, a shark? A primal, animal fear gripped Vikram. The lagoon waters abounded with fish. It wasn't safe to be swimming alone in the dark in the lagoon. As much as he regretted it, he would have to abandon the search for the board. Tinakara was his only option. He would have to swim back to the island.

The flickering light of the fire indicated where the island lay. Vikram turned towards the light and swam. Fear consumed him. The water was dark. He couldn't see. His back was stiff. What if he was bleeding? Would his blood attract sharks? There could be eels hunting in the lagoon. Their bite was terrible; they could tear out chunks of flesh. Nightmarish thoughts preyed on Vikram's mind.

A flat object loomed out of the dark. Vikram's hand struck something hard and unyielding. He shrank back, kicking wildly. His feet connected with a crumply kind of material which entangled them. Vikram writhed and thrashed, trying to free his legs. Something struck his face. Vikram reached for whatever it was. The object was rounded. He grasped it, thrusting it away. It was long and covered with a coarse material.

It was the mast of his windsurf board!

Vikram whooped with joy. Pushing the mast aside, he reached for the board. Grasping its curved edges, he dragged himself on to it. The relief that overcame him was both emotional and physical. His chest heaved. His breathing turned hard, speeding up. Tears pumped from his eyes. He pressed down on the board. He clung to it as if it was the most precious thing in his life. He swore to himself that he wouldn't lose it again. Nothing, not even the most terrifying creature of the sea would separate him from it.

Vikram lay on the board for a long time. When his nervous energy receded, he raised himself to a sitting position. He reached behind him, feeling his back. There were ridges of hardened skin there. His fingers turned sticky as he traced them. Yes, he was bleeding. He wondered what it was that had struck him. But it seemed unlikely that he would ever be able to identify the perpetrator. Some unknown creature of the sea was how he would have to leave it. He shuddered, recalling the horror of the incident. He clutched at the board, shivering. When the bout passed, he steeled himself. The horror was behind him now. He had to look ahead. It was time to resume his journey. He had to make it back to Pitti Island.

Vikram looked out across the lagoon. Nothing had changed. There was no horizon; no sign of Pitti. The only light was Basheer Koya's fire on Tinakara.

Vikram stood up and tugged the sail out of the water. The wind filled the sail and he was on his way. He pulled the sail in, turning the board to starboard. The fire and Tinakara fell behind. Vikram continued to tug at the sail till the island reverted to its original location before his fall, to his left.

Vikram held the sail tight, not wanting a repeat loss. Time passed. The wind blew steadily and Tinakara fell astern, its fire shrinking. The morning journey had been completed in little over a half-hour. If the wind held steady, he reckoned he would be in the vicinity of Pitti in twenty-five minutes.

There was a swell in the water. But it was gentle and low. Nothing to worry about. The board powered forward, trailing its green wake. Vikram was alone once more in an immense expanse of water. The darkness was foreboding yet beautiful. On the water, there wasn't much to see. But the sky dazzled with its radiance. The stars throbbed like a swarm of fireflies, stabbing the darkness with their light.

Time passed. Vikram enjoyed the journey in snatches, when the sky beguiled him with its beauty. But these moments were rare. Mostly, he scanned the darkness, searching for Pitti Island. After a long half-hour run, he dropped his sail and looked about him. If his assessment of speed and bearing were correct, he was in the vicinity of Pitti Island. But all he saw was darkness. There was no island.

Vikram resumed his search. He sailed in shorter bursts now, dropping his sail every few minutes to look. After some time, Vikram added his voice to the endeavour, shouting out Aditya and Shaukat's names. Vikram lost count of the number of times he started and stopped and shouted.

Sometime later, he switched to another part of the lagoon. Then he abandoned the new area and tried another. No one answered his calls. The darkness remained constant—immutable and unwavering.

Finally, when his voice turned hoarse, and he couldn't cry out any more, Vikram dropped his sail and sat dejectedly on the board. The crushing sensation he'd experienced when he lost his board resurfaced. He was lost. He wasn't going to find the island. His efforts, his meticulous planning were wasted. It was over.

In the far distance, Basheer Koya's fire was visible. But it was of no use to him. He had travelled too far to draw any guidance from it. Vikram wept, letting his emotions pour out of him. When the tears stopped, he hung his head in his hands and stared sightlessly at the dark water below him. He kicked his legs aimlessly. The board drifted with the currents.

Vikram looked up suddenly. He had noticed a flicker of movement in the water. He hurriedly withdrew his legs and crossed them on the board. He saw the flicker again. Something was moving in the water. He could see a shadow. The shadow had a distinct hump and it was swimming past him. Could it be a turtle? Yes, it was a turtle.

Vikram breathed easier. A turtle wouldn't harm him. He had always been soft on the creatures, and his affection had deepened after witnessing the mother turtle lay her eggs. Maybe this one was a female too, on her way to lay her eggs. Go turtle go, he cheered, go lay your eggs on an island.

Vikram caught his breath.

ISLAND!

If the turtle was on its way to lay eggs, then it was heading for an island. Might it be headed for Pitti?

Vikram rose swiftly. He reached forward to yank his sail out of the water, then halted. *Slowly*, he warned himself. *Careful*. If he alarmed the turtle, it might dive underwater and he would lose it.

The turtle was moving fast. He could see its trail by the dim phosphorescence its passage generated. He steered his board, following in the wash of the turtle.

Vikram frowned. The turtle was headed exactly opposite to where he believed the island lay.

The turtle paddled on.

Vikram sweated as he followed. He prayed that it wouldn't submerge itself and disappear underwater. Disturbing thoughts came to him. For all he knew, this turtle could be a male on a midnight forage. Or, even if it were a female, she might already have laid her eggs. If that were the case, she was headed for the reef and the deep sea.

Vikram shook his head, clearing it. This turtle was a female. She was swimming to an island to lay her eggs. That island was Pitti Island.

Vikram sailed with his heart in his mouth. The turtle seemed oblivious to his presence. It paddled steadily, as if it knew exactly where it was going. Vikram's eyes started to hurt. It was hard to see in the dark and he was straining them.

The turtle kept paddling.

Vikram grew nervous. If the turtle was headed for Pitti Island, surely it would have reached it by now.

After a while, the turtle slowed. Vikram cut his speed too, pulling in his sail. The creature's speed dropped to a crawl. Vikram panicked. Had it seen him? Was it getting ready to submerge itself?

No, the turtle's body was rising out of the water. The turtle was standing on land!

Vikram looked up. In front of him were the sharp outlines of a ring of palm trees. He could not believe it. He had found Pitti Island. A cry of victory ripped from his throat. He dropped the sail and leapt off the board. The water was not even knee-deep. He looked at the turtle. He wanted to grab it, hold it, hug it, drown it in his gratitude.

Two figures burst out from the trees shouting and running towards him. One was limping and holding back. They dashed across the sand and splashed through the water. The three friends were joyously united once again.

RETURN TO TINAKARA

Shaukat and Aditya deluged Vikram with so many questions that he flopped wearily beside the board. Half submerged in the water and interspersed with stoppages to stare lovingly at his turtle saviour, he narrated his adventure, starting with the fear he had experienced when he first spotted Basheer Koya's boats and ending finally with his harrowing journey back to Pitti.

The turtle meanwhile plodded up the beach, clearing the high-tide line.

'Wow!' said Aditya, turning to look at the reptile. 'What a story! That creature guided you home.'

'That's right,' said Vikram, staring fondly. 'Without her, I would still be out on the lagoon, hopelessly lost.'

Shaukat rose to his knees in the water. 'That was clever, Vikram. I have lived by the sea my entire life. Yet, if I were lost, the idea of tracking a turtle wouldn't have struck me. Smart thinking.' Then, still kneeling, he shuffled to Vikram's side. 'Turn around, will you?' he requested. 'Those wounds of yours. I want to have a look.'

Shaukat ran his fingers lightly over Vikram's back, tracing the gashes on his skin. He bent close, examining the injuries. After a while, he turned to Vikram, a puzzled look on his face. 'I'm not sure any fish did this to you. These are coral scars. I know because I've cut myself often on coral. You must have hit coral, brushed it more likely, when you fell into the water.'

Vikram suppressed a shudder, recalling the terror of the incident.

'You are lucky,' went on the islander. 'If you had struck the coral with more force, your back would have been a mess. You saw what happened to Aditya. You could have ended up with wounds as bad as his. You have cuts on your back, but they are manageable. I'll fix them for you.' He turned to Aditya. 'The first aid box, please.'

Aditya returned shortly with the box. Squinting in the dark, Shaukat gently applied antiseptic paste.

While Shaukat worked on his back, Vikram spoke about his plans for the night, explaining in detail how he intended to rescue Faisal and escape from Tinakara Island.

Aditya's eyes grew bigger and bigger as Vikram talked. By the time he was done, they had expanded to a size that would have done an owl proud. 'You want to travel to Tinakara on the windsurf board,' he said. 'Twice, mind you, to ferry all three of us there. Next, you want to sneak up on Basheer Koya's men and rescue Faisal. Then you want to destroy one of their boats and escape in the other. And you want us to complete all this tonight? What do you take us for, some kind of superheroes?'

Shaukat sided with Vikram. 'I don't see why it can't work,' he said. 'We'll need luck. Lots of luck, but it can work.'

'What choice do we have?' said Vikram. 'Are we going to sit around and let Faisal be taken away? Of course not. We have to try. I've thought this out. We can make it work. With luck that is, as Shaukat says.' He turned to Aditya. 'There's one thing that bothers me, and it's crucial to our plan. You are the only one who knows how to work a radio. Will you be able to manage?'

Aditya dropped his head. Kicking sand, he spoke hesitantly. 'Dad taught me how to operate his radio. I can do that. But each model is different. I don't know. It might take time to understand. I should be able to . . . but I can't give you any assurances.'

There was the matter of radio frequencies too. Aditya could not recollect his father's frequency. Knowledge of the correct frequency was vital for sending a message. But he refrained from mentioning this to his friends.

Vikram shrugged. 'Just do your best. If you get through, great. If you don't, we still have options.' He turned to Shaukat. 'Will you be able to handle the boats?'

Shaukat raised his eyebrows. 'You think I can't?' Then he laughed at Vikram's flustered expression. 'Don't worry, I can operate their boats. And I can sabotage them too. I assure you that the boat we leave behind will be of no use to them. But there's one thing you need to know. It isn't possible to navigate a boat in the dark in an unfamiliar lagoon. It's far too dangerous because the water is shallow and you have no idea where the coral lies. We will have to wait till dawn, till we can see the coral. Only then can we make our bid to escape.'

'I hadn't thought of that,' admitted Vikram. He shrugged. 'We'll wait till dawn and see what happens.'

Shaukat looked up at the stars. 'It's late. We should get moving soon.'

Vikram dropped his head. He was tired and hungry. He turned his gaze on the turtle. The reptile had huffed its way to the palm trees. It struck Vikram that the rescue mission ahead of them was going to transform their night into one as busy and as perilous as this one was for the turtle. For mother turtles, egg laying is the most dangerous endeavour of their lives, when they have to come ashore and face their worst enemy—man. Tonight, they would be facing their foes too.

Shaukat rose. 'We need two trips on the board for all of us to get to Tinakara, and that's going to take time. Come on, Aditya. I'll take you across immediately. Vikram, rest and eat in the meantime.'

Aditya reacted angrily. 'Hey!' he exclaimed. 'I'm the best windsurfer here. The fastest too. I'll take you across. And I'll return to collect Vikram.'

Vikram turned angrily on Aditya. 'Have you forgotten your injured foot?' he snapped. 'So what if you are the best windsurfer? With that foot of yours, even I'm better than you. And what about navigation? Do you think you are better than Shaukat? Will you be able to return in the dark and find Pitti? Just do what Shaukat says. We don't have time to waste.'

Vikram's outburst chastened Aditya. He walked to where the board floated and busied himself with the rigging, taking it apart and redoing it. Shaukat, meanwhile, crossed to the shelter he and Aditya had built and returned with two coconuts, which he handed to Vikram. 'Your dinner,' he smiled. 'There's coconut and fish inside. You'll like it.' Then he walked back to the shelter and after rummaging about, he reappeared with two strips of wood, which he placed on the sand. The strips were thick and sturdy and both had jagged pieces of metal screwed on at one end. 'From *Alisha*'s wreck,' he said. 'I had thought that the metal on them might be useful for us.' He grinned. 'If nothing, they'll at least come in handy as weapons.'

Vikram wondered how the rods of wood and metal would match up against machine guns. He kept silent, however, not voicing his thoughts.

They walked over to where Aditya stood beside the board.

'You sure you'll find your way back?' asked Vikram as Shaukat prepared to mount the board.

Shaukat eyes flashed in the starlight. 'I'm out at sea often at night. I know how to find my way in the dark. But just in case, if I'm not back in a couple of hours, light a fire. Keep it small. We don't want to alert Basheer Koya's men. It will help if I lose my way.'

Vikram nodded. There were no goodbyes. He watched as the wind filled the sail and the board moved forward. Aditya clung on to the tail section, his feet trailing in the water.

Darkness quickly blurred the board.

Vikram turned away. The turtle and he were the sole inhabitants of the island now. He collected his coconuts and crossed to where the animal was busy digging a hole for her eggs. He placed his meal on the sand and settled beside her.

Vikram was hungry. He hadn't eaten since breakfast. The turtle huffed and puffed at her nest as Vikram ate. Time passed. Vikram finished his meal. Then he lay on the sand and rested. Working hard, the turtle scooped sand with her flippers. When the nest was deep enough, she filled it with her eggs.

When the turtle was done and was burying her eggs, Vikram rose and stretched. It was time. Shaukat should be on his way back. He knelt beside the turtle. The animal shovelled sand, ignoring him. 'Goodbye turtle,' he whispered. 'We will never meet again, but I will remember you. Always.'

Then he rose and walked to the beach.

A brisk wind was blowing across the island. There was no sign of the fire on Tinakara, the kidnappers had probably fallen asleep. Vikram sat at the water's edge. He passed time watching hermit crabs waddle across the sand. Every now and then, he scanned the horizon for Shaukat.

He heard the board before he saw it. There was no mistaking its sound as it cut through the water at high speed. Shaukat soon materialized in front of him. Vikram waded through the water to meet him.

There was a big grin on the islander's face.

'Wow!' exclaimed Vikram. 'You found the island in the dark.'

Shaukat shrugged. 'I was lucky,' he said.

Vikram's heart warmed to his friend's modesty. Only the most talented of sailors would have found Pitti so unerringly and accurately in the dark.

There was no time to waste. Vikram clambered on to the board, his feet dragging behind him in the water. Shaukat pulled the sail and they were off.

Pitti Island fell behind and melted into the night. Vikram's feet trailed in the black unfathomable water. The sail flared above him like a manta ray floating in a black sky. A blanket of gloom surrounded them. They were sailing into a wall of blackness. Talking was difficult, and after a few attempts, they gave up. Soon Vikram's hands started to ache. His back twitched, still hurting from his wounds.

The stars twinkled coldly in the sky. There was nothing to gauge their progress by. Yet Shaukat seemed to know where they were going. Presently, he nudged Vikram with his foot. 'Tinakara,' he shouted. Vikram strained his eyes, but from where he lay all he could see was water. Soon the darkness started to wrinkle. Shadows materialized. He saw palm trees and the ghostly sliver of a beach.

Shortly after, Shaukat dropped the sail and jumped off the board. Vikram slid into the water and waded ashore. Aditya limped out of the darkness as they dragged the board on to the sand.

The greetings were brief. There was work to be done. Vikram gathered his friends around him. He explained their plan once more, detailing it from start to end.

When he was done, he turned to Aditya. 'You are going to have to behave,' he said. 'This is do-or-die stuff. Our lives and those of Faisal and Kumar depend on how we handle this. There can be no mistakes. No straying from the plan. No heroics. This is a team effort. You understand?'

Aditya placed his hand on his heart. 'Don't worry,' he said. 'I mean it. I'll be a good boy.'

The friends looked at each other. The time had come. They embraced one another and set off.

Vikram led the way. Leaving the shore, he entered the palm forest. His destination was the beach on the far side of the island. Not the spot where he had met Faisal, but further out, at the bay, where the boats were anchored. They walked slowly. Sound carried far in the silence of the night and the floor was littered with fallen palm fronds. It was warm and there was no wind under the trees. Aditya struggled. He found it hard to move silently with his injured foot.

After what seemed like ages, Vikram spotted light through the trees. The beach was near. He looked back. Shaukat had fallen behind to help Aditya. Vikram halted at the edge of the tree cover and crouched. His navigation had been spot on. He had emerged exactly where he had hoped to, right beside the boats. The tide had reversed since he had last been there. It was high now. The sea had come in and the boats were floating far from the shoreline.

Their anchor ropes creaked as they rode the swells of the lagoon. Vikram looked down the other side of the beach. A glow indicated where the fire had burnt. The outlines of the tents were visible in the distance. All was quiet. There was no sound, no movement.

Shaukat and Aditya arrived and knelt beside Vikram. Aditya dripped sweat. His breathing was loud.

'You okay?' asked Vikram.

Aditya nodded but grimaced also, and Vikram suspected he wasn't telling the truth.

'It's time to split up,' said Vikram. 'The boats are here. You two handle them. You know what to do. Faisal is my responsibility. I'll fetch him.' He turned to Shaukat. 'Can you hand me one of those clubs? I might require it.'

Shaukat wordlessly handed him one.

Vikram looked at his friends. He smiled and flashed a thumbs up sign. 'Best of luck,' he whispered and turned away.

Vikram made his way back into the tangle of palm trees. Once inside, he dropped on all fours and crept to the tents.

He heard loud snoring long before he reached them. There were shadows on the beach. Basheer Koya's men, he guessed. As he drew closer, he saw it was them, sprawled motionlessly on the sand. The tents were nearby now. Vikram searched out a spot that gave him a view of the tent Faisal shared with Kumar. He then scanned the sand around him, looking for baby coconuts. Finding several, he heaped them in a pile. Taking aim, he threw one at

Faisal's tent. It hit the canvas with an inaudible thump and fell to the ground.

The coconut and its impact went unnoticed. The men slept soundly. This was Vikram's prearranged signal with Faisal. Vikram threw a second coconut. He waited, but there was no response. Vikram bit his lip. Then he tossed another one.

Faisal was half asleep when the first coconut struck the tent. He sat up on hearing its soft plop.

Beside him, Kumar reacted too. 'Your friends,' he whispered. 'They have come.'

It was hard for Kumar to sit up as his hands and feet were both cuffed. He turned over instead and gazed at Faisal, excitement shining in his eyes.

Kumar had been in a jubilant mood ever since Faisal had told him about his meeting with Vikram. Hope had deserted him the day he had been kidnapped. And as the impending arrival of the militants had drawn near, he had sunk even deeper into despair. But Faisal's revelation had changed all that. A ray of light had shone forth. Faisal had warned him not to set his expectations too high. His friends were unarmed and outnumbered. It would be touch-and-go. Their only advantage was surprise. If their luck held, they would be freed. But Kumar hadn't cared. There was hope, and that was all that mattered.

Faisal raised his handcuffed hands and placed a finger on his lips.

Kumar nodded, a smile spreading on his face.

The second coconut bounced off the tent.

'Best of luck,' breathed Kumar as Faisal rose to his feet.

'I won't fail you,' whispered Faisal. 'You will be free soon. Goodbye.'

The third coconut hit as Faisal knelt beside the tent flap. Lifting the flap, he stepped out.

Basheer Koya's men had partied late into the night and he wasn't expecting trouble from them. In any case, if questioned, he had an answer ready—he was going to relieve himself.

Faisal stretched and yawned outside the tent. His uncle's men lay as still as boulders on the sand. Faisal scanned the trees. He saw Vikram wave and drop down. Turning, Faisal set off in his direction.

A voice spoke suddenly. 'Where are you going?' it inquired.

Faisal froze, but recovered quickly. 'Toilet,' he replied.

One of the boulders on the sand stirred and rose. It was Krishnan.

Faisal cringed inwardly. The man could ruin their plan.

'Wait a minute,' commanded Krishnan. He rubbed his eyes with one hand. His other hand rested on the barrel of his machine gun.

'I need to go to the toilet too,' he said. He rose, slinging his gun on his shoulder. 'Come, let's go.'

Faisal cursed his luck. Choosing a direction opposite to Vikram's, he walked towards the trees. The two of them relieved themselves.

Faisal had no intention of returning to the tent when he was done. Rubbing his belly, he turned to Krishnan.

'Something's wrong with my stomach,' he said. 'Getting cramps. I'm having a hard time sleeping and that damn Kumar keeps snoring.'

Krishnan smiled. 'I'm not sleepy either. Come, let's sit together.'

Faisal swore under his breath. Left with no choice, he followed the kidnapper.

Krishnan unstrapped his gun and sat on the sand. Faisal reluctantly settled himself beside the man.

The kidnapper placed the gun on his lap. 'I've been asked to keep an eye on you tonight. Your uncle has told me not to let you out of my sight.'

'He must be mad. What can I do on this island? Where can I run away to?'

'Big boss thinks you are capable of a lot of mischief. It's my job to see that you don't get up to any. This is the last night and he doesn't want any trouble.'

Faisal was out of luck. Krishnan was in an expansive mood. The kidnapper was a man who loved to talk about himself. In Faisal, he had a captive audience. Hope faded from Faisal as Krishnan broke into a long monologue about himself.

Vikram looked on in despair. Krishnan was speaking in Malayalam. He couldn't understand what the man was saying, but it was evident that his rescue attempt was on hold as long as Krishnan remained awake. The outlines of their shadows were etched sharply against the dark night sky. The machine gun on Krishnan's lap gleamed faintly.

SABOTAGE

Shaukat and Aditya watched Vikram slip away into the dark.

'Let's get moving,' said Aditya.

Shaukat looked out at the boats. 'Uh-huh,' he said. 'Not you. I will check the boats and you will stay here on shore. Don't start arguing,' he said as Aditya made to protest. 'We've discussed this before. You won't be able to move silently with your leg. You might alert someone on board and that would be the end of everything. We can't risk that happening. So you will stay here and wait for my signal.'

Aditya turned away and sat behind a palm tree.

Shaukat collected the wooden rod. 'Don't sulk,' he whispered. 'Wish me luck.'

Aditya wished him, but his tone was distinctly unenthusiastic.

Shaukat shook his head, smiling. He stole across the sand and entered the water. The beach slipped sharply beneath his feet and in two steps, he was neck-deep in cool, dark water. Kicking, he pushed off from the shore.

Shaukat swam slowly. He kept low, with just a tiny slice of his head out of the water. The shadows of the boats loomed large and soon the anchor chain of the nearer boat bobbed before him. Shaukat held it and surveyed the boat, searching for signs of human presence. No cabin lights burned, but that wasn't conclusive evidence that the boat was unmanned. Shaukat breathed deeply. Boarding the boat was going to be tricky.

He swam forward, searching for a route to the deck. On the far side of the boat, he found a ladder hanging from the railing. Stretching, he grasped it. Supporting himself on the ladder, he tucked the wooden rod into his shorts. The boat rocked as he slowly pulled himself up. He climbed the railing and dropped softly on to the deck. Water streamed from his body, splashing silently on to the steel frame of the deck. Shaukat waited, straining his ears. All he heard was the murmur of the sea and creaking of the anchor chain. There were a few crates scattered on the deck and midship there was a cabin and engine room.

Shaukat extracted the rod from his shorts and holding it, he crept towards the cabin. Steps led to a door that was open. He mounted the stairs and halting at the door, peered inside. Although he strained his eyes, he saw nothing. The cabin was darker than a cave.

Shaukat slipped inside. He smelled the familiar odour of oil and diesel. Reaching with his leg, he searched for the stairs that led to the hold. Locating them, he descended, one step at a time. It was hot. Beads of perspiration gathered on his head as he carefully lowered himself.

Suddenly, Shaukat sensed that something was wrong. He had placed his foot where the next step ought to have been, but he encountered empty space instead. He tried desperately to grab something, but it was too late; he crashed to the floor with a loud thud.

'Who's that?' shouted a startled voice in Malayalam.

Shaukat grimaced with pain. He had dropped a considerable distance, and his shoulder had slammed against the steel floor of the hold. He struggled to sit up. His shoulder was numb and the wooden rod had slipped from his hand.

A flashlight switched on, blinding him. While Shaukat blinked, someone pounced on him. Hands snaked about him, pressing him to the ground. Shaukat squirmed and heaved, trying to dislodge his assailant. But the man was strong and heavy.

Shaukat thrashed about frantically, realizing he was no match for his foe. The wooden rod. His hands scrabbled across the floor. Fingers closed in on his throat, cutting off his air supply. Shaukat grasped the man's wrists, trying to wrench them away. But it was hopeless—the man's hands were like steel. Shaukat struggled to breathe. His throat was on fire. He reached out for the man's face, poking at his eyes. His vision started to blur.

Suddenly, the pressure was released from his throat. Shaukat gasped painfully as air rushed into his lungs. He rose, clutching his throat and breathing heavily.

'You okay?' asked a familiar voice.

Shaukat looked up. A shadowy figure hovered above him.

Aditya!

The light of the torch illuminated a smile on the boy's face. In his hand was the wooden rod that Shaukat had dropped. Slumped next to Aditya was the man who had attacked Shaukat.

'What . . . what are you doing here?' breathed Shaukat.

Aditya did not reply. He averted his gaze, looking at the floor.

'Switch off the torch,' whispered Shaukat in a hoarse voice.

Aditya switched it off.

Shaukat rubbed his throat. 'Trust you to never listen to anyone. But it's a good thing you came.'

Aditya smiled in the darkness. 'Disobedience can be useful at times,' he said.

Shaukat breathed hard. There was a lot he wanted to say. But he couldn't. Aditya's warped thinking had saved the day this time. His mind reverted to the task ahead. 'Come on,' he said. 'There's no time to waste. We have to immobilize this man. There has to be rope around here. All boats carry several bundles. Switch on the torch and search. But keep it low and hood it with your hands.'

There were two bundles of rope in the hold. Aditya cut a length with his penknife, and Shaukat bound the man hand and foot. When he was done, he stuffed several dirty rags into the man's mouth.

'There's no radio on this boat,' said Aditya. He had checked the cabin and the hold while Shaukat had been busy restraining the man.

'It has to be on the other boat then,' said Shaukat. 'Come on. We should leave. Radio first. Everything afterwards.'

They climbed to the deck and squatting low looked at the shore. The beach glimmered faintly in the night light. The tents were shadows on the sand. There was no sound, no movement.

'Vikram and Faisal should have been here by now,' whispered Aditya.

Shaukat looked up at the stars. Jupiter was low on the horizon. There wasn't much time for daybreak, an hour at the most.

'Something's holding them up. But let's not worry about them. We have work to do.'

They slipped into the water and swam to the other boat. Shaukat carried the torch, keeping it dry above his head. Aditya paddled with the wooden rod in his hand. Locating the ladder, they pulled themselves on board. They crouched in the darkness and listened intently. There was no sound.

Shaukat brought his hands to his lips. He gestured, indicating that Aditya should stay while he checked the boat. Aditya nodded. Shaukat crept up the stairs and entered the cabin.

Aditya waited outside, ready to rush in at the slightest sound. The boat rocked gently as the tide tugged at it. The minutes ticked by. Aditya clenched his weapon. He had heard sounds of movement inside.

A shadow appeared. 'Don't hit me,' whispered Shaukat. 'It's okay. There's no one on board. Come on in.'

Inside the cabin, Shaukat switched on the flashlight, hooding it with his fingers. 'There's the radio,' he said.

At the front of the cabin stood a raised platform with a pilot wheel attached to it. To one side, there was a flat desk-like structure with a radio installed on it. Aditya sat on the chair beside it. He breathed a sigh of relief when he saw that it was a standard design machine. There were the usual controls of the PTT button, the mike and dials for setting frequencies.

Shaukat stood beside Aditya, illuminating the machine with the torch. 'Think you can handle it?' he asked.

Aditya sucked a breath. 'It looks okay. It should work, but I'm not guaranteeing anything.' He fiddled with the knobs. 'We have another problem. One we hadn't thought of. This radio's going to hiss and crackle and on a quiet night like this, the sound will carry to the shore. It's possible that the men might hear it.'

'Hmm,' said Shaukat. He thought for a while. Then he nodded. 'I'll have to release the anchor. That's the only way. The boat will drift when it's free. The tide is moving out and it will carry the boat with it. Give it fifteen minutes and we should be far enough for you to start transmitting. You'll have time to familiarize yourself with the radio by then.' Shaukat straightened himself. 'I had better leave now. I'll release our anchor first. Then I'll work on the other boat. It shouldn't take long to sabotage it.' Shaukat made for the cabin door, then halted. A frown creased his face.

Aditya guessed what was troubling him. 'It's Vikram and Faisal, isn't it?'

Shaukat nodded. He stepped out on to the deck. Aditya followed him. They bent low, crouching behind the railing. The tents shimmered in the dark. The beach was silent and empty. There was no sign of Vikram and Faisal.

'They should have been here long ago,' murmured Shaukat.

'They haven't been captured,' said Aditya. 'That's for sure. The beach would have been swarming with men, if it were so.'

'That's right,' said Shaukat. 'But what's holding them back? The later they escape, the more difficult it will get for them. The boat will drift once I release the anchor. They will have to swim out far to get to us, and for Faisal, it will be even harder. His hands are cuffed.'

'I hadn't thought of that,' said Aditya. 'What do we do then? Do we leave the anchor where it is?'

Shaukat shook his head. 'No. We can't wait. The radio is more important. It's what really matters. If you get the message out, our job is done.' He turned to Aditya. 'Go on inside. I'm releasing the anchor. Start transmitting the moment you feel we've drifted far enough. I'll join you once I'm done with the other boat.'

Aditya embraced Shaukat and returned to the cabin.

Shaukat went over to the aft section of the boat. The anchor winch was near the railing. Crouching beside it, he removed the cover. The chain was wound around a spindle. Working quickly, he unwound it. When he reached the end of the chain, he unclipped it and dropped it in the water. Instantly, there was a change in the boat's motion, a perceptible sense of drift. The tide had caught the boat and was dragging it along.

The first task was done. Next, he had to sabotage the other boat. Shaukat entered the water, swam to the other boat and ascended its ladder.

Crossing to the aft end of this boat, he unwound the anchor chain as before and dropped it into the water. Next, Shaukat searched for a bucket and found one nearby, fastened to a rubber water tank. He freed the bucket, filled it with water from the tank and entered the dark cabin. The starlight filtering through the cabin windows wasn't strong enough to light the hold and engine area. But Shaukat had inspected the hold earlier with the knocked-out kidnapper's torch and was confident he could find his way around.

Moving carefully, he descended the stairs. He could hear the steady breathing of the immobilized man. The well of the boat was dark and Shaukat had to feel his way about. It didn't take him long to find the engine and his questing fingers sought out the dipstick, which was used to measure the oil level inside the engine. He pulled it out and dropped it to the ground. Then he picked up the bucket and holding it over the dipstick hole, he poured the water down the hole into the engine. When the bucket emptied, he returned to the deck, refilled the bucket and poured water into the engine once more. After repeating the manoeuvre five times, he was done. He replaced the dipstick in its hole and climbed to the deck.

While refilling the bucket, Shaukat had spied a metal cupboard with a set of spanners screwed on to it.

Shaukat unfastened the smaller spanners and placed them in his pocket. The engine exhaust pipe was nearby. It rose vertically, topping out at the cabin roof level. There was a steel ladder beside the exhaust pipe. Shaukat climbed it till he was level with the top of the exhaust pipe. Reaching out, Shaukat placed his hands on the pipe, locating its mesh covering. He unfastened the cover and tossed it aside. Then he extracted the spanners from his pockets and dropped them inside.

Shaukat grinned as he descended to the deck. The water he had poured into the engine would cause it to cease shortly after it was started. The spanners were an additional surety. They would damage the machine's internal mechanism.

Pleased with himself, Shaukat halted at the railing. Aditya's boat was nearby; the tide was carrying the boats together. He lowered himself into the water and swam to the other boat. Aditya was peering at the radio with the flashlight when he entered the cabin. A pair of headphones and a bundle of wires were lying at his feet.

Aditya looked up. 'Everything okay?' he asked.

'Mission accomplished,' nodded Shaukat. 'Any sign of Vikram?'

Aditya fiddled with the headphones. 'I can't understand why he hasn't shown up.'

Shaukat stared at Aditya. Then he knelt, scrutinizing the radio. 'Any progress?' he asked.

'Everything's okay with the machine. I will be able to operate it.' He paused. 'The only problem is the frequency.'

'What do you mean?'

'Dad and all the other pilots operate on a particular frequency. If I want to send a message to him, it has to be on that frequency, otherwise he won't receive it.'

'So?'

Aditya dropped his head. 'I've forgotten the frequency,' he said.

Shaukat placed a hand on Aditya's shoulder. 'There are other frequencies, aren't there? The navy would have one, other ships have them . . . How do you send out SOS and Mayday calls?'

'There are international distress frequencies, but I don't know them.'

'Then you have to remember your father's frequency. Think . . . It's our only hope.'

Aditya stared at the radio. While Shaukat had been busy sabotaging the other boat, Aditya had dug deep into his memory and after much thought had settled finally on a range. His father's frequency was above 10,000 kHz, he was sure about that. And without being able to pinpoint why, he was certain it was below 11,000 kHz. But 1000 kHz was a large range. His father had said that a frequency setting has to be precise; at the most, an overlap of 3–4 kHz is permissible. If the operator is off by more, the message will be inaudible.

'Dad's frequency is between 10,000 and 11,000 kHz,' said Aditya. He gestured with his hands. 'It could be anywhere between those limits. My plan is to transmit within that range. I'll keep changing the frequency and repeating my message over and over again. Hopefully, one of the transmissions will be at the correct frequency.'

'Then what are you waiting for?' cried Shaukat. 'We are far from the shore now. No one will hear. Start. Don't waste time.'

Aditya turned to the radio.

Shaukat stepped out on to the deck.

The sky was streaked with ribbons of red. Shadowed trees were visible in the strengthening light. The shoreline had slipped far away. The tents were faint white spots on the shore. Shaukat surveyed the scene with a heavy heart. It was clear that they would have to abandon Vikram and Faisal.

From behind him, the buzz of static and disturbance wafted out as Aditya switched on the radio.

187

UNDER FIRE

Krishnan was in an expansive mood. Among his friends, the hoodlum had a reputation of being a blabbermouth—particularly late at night after downing several drinks, when he tended to ramble endlessly about himself. His companions shunned him on such occasions, but on that night, in Faisal, he had found the perfect audience.

Poor Faisal. There was little he could do. He was forced to sit while Krishnan launched a garbled, disjointed monologue about himself. He longed to get away. Vikram was waiting for him in the trees. Shaukat and Aditya must be worrying about them. And Kumar, what must he be thinking? The man had staked all his hopes on him.

Vikram fretted too. Precious time was slipping by. But the kidnapper was armed. There was nothing he could do.

On the beach, Krishnan was busy chronicling his life history. It was a long and gory tale about how he had become a gang leader and an underworld king.

Faisal paid little attention to Krishnan. As time went on, a feeling of hopelessness descended on the boy. It was clear that the kidnapper had no intention of letting up.

As the stars faded overhead, Vikram came to a decision. He couldn't sit by and let one man ruin their plans. Yes, Krishnan had a machine gun. It was because of the gun that he had held back, but now his hand was being forced. It was time to act. He fingered the jagged pieces of metal on his wooden club. The weapon was as good as any. Holding the club in his hand, he crept forward.

Krishnan sat with his back to Vikram. The sky lightened overhead as Vikram crawled towards the man. The stars dimmed and winked out one by one. If Vikram had cared to look at the lagoon, he would have noticed that the boats had drifted far from the shore. Vikram crawled fast. Krishnan was so into his storytelling that he did not expect the hoodlum to be even remotely aware of his approach. Finally, he reached striking distance, but a fallen palm frond blocked his progress. Vikram raised himself.

Faisal had spotted the two boats drifting a long while ago. Not wanting Krishnan to notice them, he pretended to pay attention.

Krishnan was saying: '. . . I was forced to leave Cochin when I killed a rival gang leader.' He smiled crookedly. 'I had to skip town after that. The man had connections. I left town on one of the boats at the docks. The boat belonged to your uncle. That was how I met him. Your uncle is a leader of men. I decided to work with him and I haven't looked back since. He has taught me a lot. He can be a terrifying man when he wants to. I have never met anybody so ruthless.' Krishnan looked keenly at Faisal. 'You are in trouble, young man. I don't see how your uncle can let you go free. You know too . . .' Krishnan stopped mid-sentence. He had spotted the drifting boats. Swearing loudly, he started to rise.

Faisal groaned silently. As he reached out to pull Krishnan back, he saw a shadow rise from behind. Krishnan heard something and started to turn. Vikram swung hard, cracking his club on Krishnan's head. The crunch of rod on the skull rang sharply in the still of the morning. Faisal caught Krishnan as he sagged. They crouched in the sand, waiting to see if any of the sleeping men had been roused. But the only sound was their own quickened breathing.

Vikram eased the machine gun from Krishnan's grasp. The kidnapper lay face down in the sand. Faisal asked Vikram to flip the man over. Vikram was puzzled, but he complied. Faisal extended his handcuffed hands to Krishnan's shirt pocket. He searched briefly and withdrew his hands with a bunch of keys dangling from his fingers. Vikram quickly fitted one in Faisal's cuffs and unlocked them.

A smile lit Faisal's features as the handcuffs dropped to the sand. He embraced Vikram. Then he requested him for the keys.

Vikram looked at him.

'Kumar,' whispered Faisal. 'I can free him with the keys.'

'Can he swim?' asked Vikram as he handed them over. 'Look where the boats are.'

'The boats are too far to swim to,' breathed Faisal. 'We'll have to take the dinghy. It's parked right here.'

Vikram stared. Then he nodded. 'Great idea,' he said. 'Get Kumar. I'll wait by the dinghy.'

Faisal departed.

Vikram glanced at Krishnan. His eyes were closed, his face half in the sand. Faisal's discarded handcuffs lay nearby. Vikram slipped them around Krishnan's wrists and clicked them into place.

The sun was peeping over the horizon, its rays colouring the sand orange. Vikram bent low. Clutching the machine gun, he stole across the sand to the dinghy. The rubber boat floated in the water, fastened to a pole buried in the sand. Vikram yanked the pole out of the sand and placed it inside the dinghy along with the machine gun. He towed the boat out till the water was thigh-deep. Holding the starter cord in his hand, he faced the shore.

Inside the tent, Kumar was wide awake. Faisal swiftly unlocked his cuffs.

Kumar leapt upright, his eyes shining like stars.

'Come,' whispered Faisal. 'We must leave now. Follow me.'

They slid quietly from the tent. Faisal led the way to the dinghy. He moved swiftly, padding noiselessly past the sleeping men. Kumar followed, limping and shuffling at a slower pace. The Tamilian was struggling. Having been shackled for days on end, his feet weren't coordinating properly.

Kumar halted. It was no use. He couldn't keep up with Faisal. Looking up, he saw a boy standing beside a dinghy in the water. The boy was waving, signalling him to hurry. Kumar surveyed the beach. There were several men on the sand. He would have to pass them to get to the dinghy. Faisal had already done so and was waiting at the water's edge.

No matter the condition of his legs, Kumar had to hurry. Step by agonizing step, he worked his way forward. It was when he was passing the last kidnapper that he slipped and fell to the ground.

The man sat up. 'Idiot!' he swore. 'Can't you see where you are going?'

Kumar staggered to his feet and sprinted on wobbly legs to the dinghy.

A yell of alarm pierced the morning stillness.

'Stop them, they are escaping!' screamed the hoodlum, wide awake now.

Discarding all pretence of silence, Kumar ran forward. Vikram yanked the starter and the motor roared to life. Faisal leapt on board and grabbed the throttle.

The beach had sprung to life. Three men were hotly in pursuit of Kumar. Others were sitting up and calling out to one another.

Faisal and Vikram shouted, urging Kumar on. When finally he splashed into the water, Vikram extended a hand and pulled him aboard. Faisal engaged the engine and the boat surged forward, leaving the sprinting men behind. A pistol shot rang out. It was followed immediately by another.

Vikram and Faisal crouched in the boat. In the melee and excitement, Vikram had forgotten about the machine gun.

He reached for it, only to find that Kumar had already grabbed it. The man stooped low, the gun at his waist. The machine gun chattered loudly as he sprayed a burst across the beach. Vikram watched in fascination as the beach cleared in an instant, the kidnappers dropping to the sand. Kumar fired a second burst, raking the shore with bullets.

The dinghy sped forward, making for the drifting boats.

Shaukat's heart was sinking with each passing moment. It was dawn and there was still no sign of Vikram or Faisal. Even if they appeared now, it was too late. The boats had drifted. The distance was too far to swim.

It was down to the radio now. Only the radio could save them.

The machine was hissing and the crackling in the cabin and Aditya was speaking into it.

'SOS, SOS. This is Aditya Khan calling. We are marooned on the Tinakara-Pitti Islands. We are in trouble. Anybody hearing this message, please contact the navy or the helicopter pilots immediately. We need rescue. Repeat, we are on the Tinakara-Pitti Islands and need immediate rescue.'

Aditya recited the message over and over again. Between each transmission, he would turn a knob, tweak the frequency and speak again.

On the deck, Shaukat suddenly jerked upright. A sputtering sound had penetrated the whine and static of the radio. It was the noise of an engine. Shaukat stared at the shore. A dinghy was floating in the water. Two shadows were crouched on board, and a third was rushing forward.

Vikram and Faisal!

Why had they started the dinghy? Didn't they know that the noise would rouse everybody on the island? Who was the man running towards them?

Aditya arrived breathlessly at Shaukat's side.

The man boarded the dinghy and the vessel shot away from the shore. Shaukat and Aditya froze as a shot rang out and then another.

Aditya yelled in glee as Kumar sprayed the shore with bullets. He turned to Shaukat. 'Don't just stand there,' he yelled. 'Start the engine. They will be here soon. Get the boat ready.'

Shaukat tore himself from the unfolding drama and dashed into the cabin.

The gunfire ceased. The dinghy roared forward.

Aditya felt the boat shudder as Shaukat switched on the engine.

Vikram, too, heard the boat start. He could see Aditya waving from the deck of the boat.

Faisal raced the dinghy in a curve towards the protected side of the boat—its starboard side—which was invisible from the shore.

Aditya understood Faisal's ploy and dashed through the cabin to the starboard side, passing Shaukat who was standing at the wheel.

'Let me know when everybody is on board,' yelled Shaukat as Aditya flew past him.

Machine gun fire erupted again—this time from the island. Glass tinkled and exploded as bullets embedded themselves in the boat.

Aditya crouched. He was safe. The bullets would have to bore their way through the boat to get to him.

On the water, Faisal—waving joyfully at Aditya—brought the dinghy in, manoeuvring it parallel to the starboard railing.

Aditya made a fist and waved his hand too.

In the cabin, Shaukat bent low as bullets whistled around him. He cried in anguish when bullets thudded into the radio, extinguishing its buzz and static.

Aditya threw a rope to Faisal who tied it to the dinghy as it came to rest by the side of the boat. Faisal sprang nimbly on board. Vikram and Kumar followed. Aditya yelled to Shaukat to get moving.

The boat lurched forward. Shaukat was having a hard time. The hail of bullets forced him to crouch under the wheel. He couldn't see where they were going. Steering blind in a coral-filled lagoon was stupid. It wouldn't do. He would have to stand up. But the stream of bullets ensured that he couldn't. He abandoned the wheel and crawled to the starboard deck, yelling for Faisal.

Bullets slapped relentlessly into the boat. Faisal wriggled across the deck towards Shaukat, a big grin on his face. The friends embraced. Shaukat then requested Faisal to sit at the starboard prow of the boat—where he would be safe from bullets—and pass him instructions for navigating the boat through the coral.

At the aft end of the boat, Kumar lay sprawled on the deck, trading bullets with the gunman on shore. During a break, Kumar spotted men in the water, swimming to the boat Shaukat had sabotaged. He fired a sharp burst, forcing them back to the shore.

Kumar turned his attention to Basheer Koya's tent. The machine gun was being operated from there. He let fly a long burst at the tent. There was silence as the gun stopped firing. Kumar grinned in satisfaction. He stood up, but a hail of machine gun fire sent him crashing back to the deck.

The cabin was a mess. Shattered glass lay everywhere. The entire frame of the windshield had disintegrated. Shaukat hunched low under the wheel. Beside him crouched Vikram, half in and half out of the cabin. From outside, Faisal shouted steering instructions to Vikram, and Vikram relayed them to Shaukat.

Faisal was an expert at spotting coral. But under the circumstances, crouched to avoid the gunfire, his vision was limited to a few metres, which was inadequate for steering a fast-moving craft.

Shaukat sweated at the wheel. He wished he could open the throttle and speed the boat out of machine gun range, but he restrained himself. Crashing into coral could have worse consequences than damage wrought by bullets.

At the rear end of the boat, Kumar decided to hold his fire. His ammunition was limited and could run out any moment. Basheer Koya evidently had no such problem. His gun continued to chatter, raking the boat with sharp bursts.

The boat moved at a crawl, Shaukat painstakingly following the directions Vikram relayed to him.

The machine gun suddenly stopped chattering.

'They are reloading their gun,' shouted Kumar. He fired a warning burst to dissuade anybody from entering the water.

Faisal rose to his feet. His instructions to Shaukat were precise now and the boat picked up speed. The coral outcroppings were a dark shade of green in the turquoise waters of the lagoon. The exit passage from the lagoon wasn't far. Faisal could see it. Two large clumps of coral lay in between barring their way to the passage. Shaukat, who was standing now, could also see the approaching coral.

A hail of bullets swept the boat, forcing Shaukat to throw himself to the deck.

'Starboard,' yelled Faisal frantically. 'Hard to starboard.'

But Shaukat was in no position to respond. He had dived on glass and had cut himself. The wheel spun out of control.

'Right, right,' screamed Faisal.

There was a bone-jarring thud accompanied with screech of metal tearing into living coral. The boat lurched to a halt. Shaukat grabbed frantically at the wheel, bullets screaming around him. He tugged hard, but the boat did not respond. Shaukat doubled his efforts.

A fast-moving swell caught the boat. The vessel shuddered, struggling to break free from the unforgiving grasp of the coral. Seconds later, another swell lifted the boat. Metal grated on coral and suddenly, it floated free.

The boat limped towards the exit channel, the swells of the open sea pushing it forward.

Faisal could sense something was wrong. 'Hold steady!' he shouted as the boat ploughed into the waves. Shaukat struggled at the wheel. The boat responded sluggishly, he couldn't hold her steady.

Kumar lay sprawled on the rear deck. He had been peeping over the railing the past few minutes, trying to locate the machine gun. By the time the boat stuttered out of the lagoon, he had estimated that it was being fired from behind a bush to one side of the tents. Taking aim, he unleashed a long burst. The chatter of the shore gun abruptly ceased.

THE MILITANTS

It was finally calm on the deck. Bullets were no longer slapping into the boat and ricocheting everywhere. Aditya sprang to his feet and ran to the radio. Vikram joined him and placed a commiserating arm on his shoulder when he saw the condition of the machine. There wasn't much left of it. A bullet had gone right through the radio, carving it into two pieces. An assortment of other bullets had ripped the controls apart.

Aditya had a haunted look on his face.

'You're not sure whether you got through, are you?' asked Vikram.

'The message went out.' Aditya breathed hard. 'I must have sent it a hundred times. But the frequency was random. The navy or my dad might have received it . . . or, they might not have.' Aditya stared at the destroyed machine. 'I . . . I don't know.'

'A hundred times!' Vikram slapped Aditya on his back. 'That's a lot. Why are you looking like the world had ended? Someone will have heard. Don't worry.'

Outside, the morning light had strengthened and the sky had turned blue. Vikram saw that they were out of the lagoon. The white line that marked the reef was behind them now.

A fresh burst of machine gun fire sent both Vikram and Aditya diving to the cabin floor again.

At the aft end of the boat, Kumar had been waiting for the shooting to resume. Peering over the railing, he estimated where the bullets were being fired from and triggered a long burst. But midway through, his bullets stopped and although Kumar pressed the trigger repeatedly, all he heard was empty clicking noises. His ammunition had run out.

Up front, Faisal crouched on the prow of the boat. He was no longer being called upon for steering assistance. The danger was behind them. They had exited the treacherous coral zone and were now in the deep waters of the Arabian Sea. Yet, in spite of their escape, Faisal was worried. The boat was heeling too far to port. The impact of the coral weighed on his mind. Had the collision damaged the vessel?

Tinakara Island fell astern. The machine gun continued to spit fury from the shore, but the bullets were no longer reaching them. Soon they could move without fear on the deck. Faisal went to where he had lashed the dinghy and inspected it. Shielded by the hull of the vessel, the rubber boat had survived the onslaught of bullets.

Shaukat summoned everybody to the cabin. Kumar tramped in last, ducking as he entered through the door.

Vikram had helped rescue the man, but it was only now that he noted his features. Kumar was dark-skinned and tall, topping Aditya by half a head. He was young, his hair wavy and dark, with no trace of white in it. He stood beside Aditya, crouching to accommodate his head under the cabin roof.

The strained look on Shaukat's face put an end to Vikram's triumphant mood. It was clear something was wrong.

Faisal spoke first. 'There's a problem with the boat, isn't there?'

Shaukat nodded. 'The coral has damaged her,' he said in a heavy voice. 'I'm doing all I can to stop her from going round in circles.'

The news dismayed everyone. Kumar's distress was the strongest.

'No!' he cried. 'We have to get away. I don't want to fall into the hands of the militants. They have sworn to kill me.'

Shaukat raised a pacifying hand. 'It's not over yet. We might still get away. The boat is managing some kind of headway.'

Kumar pointed through the shattered window at the Tinakara lagoon. 'That other boat of theirs,' he said. 'It will run us down in no time.'

'The boat has been taken care of.' A smile played on Shaukat's lips. 'The engine will break down the moment they start it. You don't have to worry about Basheer Koya any more. He and his men are no longer a threat. It's our boat that is the problem. Our rudder might be damaged. I'm hoping it isn't. It's possible that something is stuck down there. We'll swim down and check. For that I'll have to switch off the engine. Faisal, I want you to dive and inspect the rudder.'

Shaukat switched off the engine. In the silence, they heard the sea and the slap of the waves on the hull. No longer powered, the boat started to pitch and roll.

Aditya accompanied Faisal to the front deck. He cheered him on when he jumped overboard and disappeared under the boat.

Vikram spotted a pair of binoculars hanging on the cabin wall. They had miraculously survived the barrage of bullets. Picking them up, he walked, out on to the swaying deck.

Pitti Island slipped into focus first when Vikram adjusted the binoculars. Although the island was distant, he could clearly see its palm trees and the strip of sand circling it. Vikram blinked. Pitti seemed unreal. An oasis of peace and calm—so far removed from the tension and fear aboard the boat. Vikram gazed longingly at it, wishing he was there.

Balancing on the heaving deck, he trained the binoculars next on Tinakara. Basheer Koya's men had split up into two groups—one set on the beach, the others on board the abandoned boat. Vikram focused his glasses on the boat. He saw men inside its cabin. It was hard to tell, but they seemed to be arguing and gesticulating. Vikram stared at the cabin for a long time. The men continued to chatter and wave their hands. Vikram grinned. Shaukat had successfully sabotaged the vessel. Basheer Koya and his men were no longer a threat.

Bracing himself, he turned the binoculars away, scanning the sea. Moments later, he froze. He blinked, wishing the apparition he saw would disappear. But it didn't. It held fast instead, magnified several times by the binoculars.

A boat.

Vikram gripped the binoculars hard. The militants! It could only be them.

Faisal, meanwhile, had surfaced and clambered up the ladder. He halted beside Shaukat and shook his head. 'It's no use. The rudder's gone. It's broken and can't be fixed.'

Kumar grasped Shaukat's shoulders. 'But we can still run the boat like before, can't we?'

Shaukat kept silent. He dropped his head.

Vikram spoke up. 'Sorry friends, but there's more bad news.' He turned and pointed. The militant boat was clearly visible, a rounded blip on the dark blue sea.

Everybody stared. The significance of the boat's presence shook them. All escape avenues were cut off. Their fate was sealed. The militants could pick them up at their leisure.

But Faisal hadn't lost hope. 'Why are we standing here like statues? We still have the dinghy. Let's go!'

Everyone sprang to action. Shaukat issued instructions. 'Faisal, you and Aditya load a fuel drum into the dinghy. Vikram, you and Kumar search for food and water. Take along whatever you find. Come on. There's no time to waste.'

Everyone went about their tasks. A fuel drum, two jerrycans of water and food were lowered on to the dinghy. Shaukat took care not to overload the boat. Speed was of the essence. In flat, calm water, the dinghy could move faster than a boat, but in the deep, heaving sea, big boats fared better. The militants would outrun them. Their best hope was a good head start. Unlike a boat, the dinghy rode low on the water. If they managed to disappear over the horizon, it would be hard for the militants to spot them.

They quickly boarded the dinghy and cast off.

Shaukat pointed the boat away from the islands and opened the throttle wide. The dinghy leapt forward, cutting speedily through the water.

Captain Abbas Khan slept fitfully in the radio room at the Kalpeni Naval Base.

He had flown to Kalpeni the day the boys had been reported missing and had been camping there since, heading the naval search for the missing *Alisha*.

The search had begun the moment the weather had settled. Captain Khan had flown from sunrise to sunset each day, halting only when there was no light to search by. The rescue effort had been concentrated north of Kalpeni, around the area where the sandbanks lay, as this was where the boys had said they were going. Two helicopters had flown twelve hours a day, halting only to refuel and then flying on again. Scanning the boundless expanse of the ocean for a tiny boat was a tiresome task. Captain Khan's eyes ached from the strain of endlessly searching the sunlit waters. The days had passed with no sign of the boat. Hope had started to fade, but Captain Khan refused to give in.

He always slept in the radio room, in the faint hope that some passing ship would find the boys and radio in to Kalpeni. It was a forlorn gesture, but Captain Khan was unwilling to believe that the boys were lost.

The day, like the earlier ones, had been long and tiring. Captain Khan dosed fitfully next to the radio. Mr Singh, his co-pilot and friend, slept next to him. Mr Singh had been a revelation the past few days, exhibiting loyalty and friendship of a high order. Night and day, he had made himself available for Captain Khan, standing rocklike by his captain, a solid shoulder for him to lean on.

The radio made noises, hissing like a cooker in the room. Towards morning, Captain Khan turned increasingly restless, and shortly before dawn, he sat up in bed, resting his head against the wall. He was in this position when Aditya's message crackled across the ether.

'SOS, SOS, this is Aditya Khan calling.' On hearing the word, 'SOS', Captain Khan sprang across the room with a leap that would have done an athlete proud. Grabbing the volume knob, he turned it to its highest, rousing Mr Singh. The message that shrilled through was neither clear nor strong.

'We are . . . Tinakara Island. We are in trouble. Anybody hearing . . . please contact . . . pilots . . . need immediate . . . Repeat, we are on Tinakara-Pitti . . . rescue.'

Aditya was alive!

A cry rose from deep within Captain Khan.

When the message ended, Captain Khan pressed the PTT button. 'Aditya! Aditya, my son, I am coming right away. Don't worry, I will be there. Is everything all right? How are you? How are the others?'

'Easy, sir,' cautioned Mr Singh who was crouched beside him. 'One question at a time.'

Captain Khan pressed the PTT button once more. 'What is the matter, Aditya? Why don't you reply?'

There was no response, only the hiss of static.

Mr Singh eased the PTT button from Captain Khan's hands and pressed. 'Aditya,' he said, 'You are at Tinakara Island. Is that right?'

The response was no different. Only static.

Captain Khan turned to his co-pilot, his eyes bright like the morning sun. 'It was Tinakara! Both of us heard him. He said he needed rescue. Come on.'

They were ready in minutes. Mr Singh grabbed his turban as they rushed across the helipad to their machine.

The helicopter was quickly airborne. Inside the cabin, Captain Khan set course for Tinakara while Mr Singh transmitted their flight details to the naval headquarters at Kavaratti Island.

Dawn was streaking the skies. The light quickly brightened and the sea changed colour from black to grey and finally to a deep blue. Captain Khan gazed at the horizon, impatiently awaiting the appearance of the islands.

RESCUE

The dinghy leapt from swell to swell. The Tinakara-Pitti Islands had long fallen below the horizon. Even the boat they had abandoned had disappeared.

The boys kept a keen lookout for the militants' boat. Would it appear and drown their hopes, or would they have time to lose themselves in the vast expanse of the ocean?

Shaukat sat with his hands on the throttle. The others had spread themselves across the length of the dinghy, squatting amidst the water-cans and the fuel drum.

Tension pressed like a cloud on the boat. Kumar bit his nails fearfully, glancing continuously over his shoulder. Aditya played with the empty machine gun. Vikram and Faisal stared at the rolling blue waters around them.

Disturbed by the passage of the dinghy, flying fish leapt continuously from the water. They flew at wave top level, gliding long distances before diving head first into the water. Vikram likened them to grasshoppers. On land, grasshoppers did the same, jumping out of the way and losing themselves immediately after. Flying fish were the grasshoppers of the sea.

After an hour, their fuel ran out. Faisal and Shaukat quickly transferred fuel from the drum to the motor tank. Aditya stood up, supporting himself on Vikram's shoulder. Shading his eyes, he stared back along the way they had come. It was impossible to guess in which direction Tinakara lay. Everywhere around them was featureless blue sea. But there was a discontinuity in the distance. A faraway speck. 'Oh no!' breathed Aditya. The speck on the horizon was a boat. Vikram saw Aditya turn rigid. Kumar stared. As if by telepathy, everyone knew what Aditya had seen.

The militants had established eye contact. Escape was impossible now. Capture was only a matter of time.

Refuelling completed, Faisal started the engine. The dinghy resumed its journey. Nobody spoke. They waited silently for the inevitable. In the vast emptiness that surrounded them, there was no place to hide.

The helicopter droned over the sea. The pilots were familiar with the monotonous view below. Only this time there was no straining of eyes, no scanning the water. This wasn't a search mission. They were flying to a fixed destination—the Tinakara-Pitti Islands.

Although there was a great happiness inside Captain Khan, he was disturbed too. Why hadn't Aditya replied? There was also the matter of the tone of his message. Despite travelling to the ionosphere and back, the raw tension in his voice had come through. And why the word, 'immediate'? Why had he requested immediate help? Was something wrong? Was he hurt?

Mr Singh was the first to notice the islands. He nudged his senior partner and pointed. The islands were barely visible, a puckering of the sea in the distance.

The puckering expanded, spreading in a turquoise stain. Soon the islands took shape and palm trees waved at them. Mr Singh pointed once more. There was a boat in the water. It was a biggish boat, larger than a standard fishing vessel. It was travelling fast, spewing a frothing trail.

Captain Khan disengaged the autopilot and banked the helicopter, steering for the boat. Could Aditya and his friends be on board? It was possible, reasoned Captain Khan. The Tinakara-Pitti Islands were uninhabited. There was no radio on the islands. Maybe Aditya had transmitted his message from the boat's radio.

The boat was a large trawler. As they drew near, the trawler changed course, veering sharply to port. Captain Khan was taken aback. Why would a boat execute such a dramatic change in course, especially at a high speed?

The helicopter descended and flew low over the boat. Several bare-chested men in bright lungis waved at the pilots. There was nothing suspicious about the vessel. It appeared to be a regular native craft out on a fishing trip. The boys weren't on board the trawler. Captain Khan executed a tight circle around the boat, and then pointed his aircraft at the islands.

The sea changed from blue to turquoise as they crossed the reef and flew over the lagoon. Captain Khan handed the controls to his co-pilot and studied the islands. The small circular island directly beneath was Pitti. The island carried the scars the storm had inflicted on it. Captain Khan saw a tangle of palm trees and a ring of shining sand.

Pitti Island lay near the edge of the lagoon. The froth of waves breaking against the reef was visible. Captain Khan drew a sharp breath. There was something in the water close to the reef. Mr Singh had seen the submerged object too. He turned the helicopter and hovered above it.

The wreck of the *Alisha* lay beneath them. Although he couldn't identify the wreckage, Captain Khan instinctively knew he was staring down on the *Alisha*.

If the boys were not on this island, they had to be on the other.

The helicopter covered the distance between Pitti and Tinakara in less than a minute. There was a boat in the sheltered bay at Tinakara. Another identical boat floated outside the lagoon, dangerously close to the reef.

There were people on the island.

Mr Singh flew low, skimming the beach. Men waved at the helicopter as it flew past. No sign of Aditya and the boys. It was all very puzzling. They circled the island.

On the far side of Tinakara Island, Captain Khan spotted an abandoned windsurf board. He exulted. There wasn't a shadow of doubt now that the boys had come to these islands.

But where were they?

Captain Khan instructed his co-pilot to circle the island again. When they approached the sheltered bay, he requested his junior to make for the boat floating outside the reef. The turquoise water of the lagoon flashed below them and soon they were hovering above the boat. There was no one on board. The boat had been abandoned. It was floating free and was in imminent danger of being swept on to the reef.

Captain Khan scratched his head. He couldn't make head or tails of what he was seeing. The boys had come here. That was for sure. But there was no sign of them. The men on shore would know. It was best to talk to them. Captain Khan requested his pilot to land the helicopter.

Mr Singh climbed high, searching for a place to land.

The boys were in their dinghy, and all but impossible to spot on the boundless expanse of the sea. There had been great jubilation when the helicopter had appeared. Kumar had broken into a war dance. Aditya had beamed with happiness. Everybody had hugged and congratulated him. His message had gone through.

They had yelled and danced, almost capsizing the dinghy. The helicopter—a naval one—passed them on their starboard side, heading for the militants' boat. They saw it circle the boat and fly away. Doubts crept into their minds as they watched it make for the islands.

Had the helicopter come searching for them? Or was it on a routine flight?

Whatever the helicopter's mission, it was obvious they hadn't been spotted. Their elation evaporated. Despair returned. Returned to all . . . all except Shaukat. Shaukat wasn't in the least disturbed that the helicopter had overflown them. He had anticipated this. Shaukat understood the vast expanse of the sea and the near impossibility of locating a speck like a dinghy on its surface. Earlier, on board the boat they had abandoned, while the others had loaded the dinghy, Shaukat had searched the cabin for flares. Most sea-going vessels carry emergency flares and luckily for him, Basheer Koya's vessel had them. Shaukat had transferred the flares to the dinghy and tucked them away in a side pocket.

Now, while the others breathlessly watched, Shaukat extracted a flare and ignited it.

Hovering high over Tinakara Island, both Captain Khan and Mr Singh saw the bright orange flame.

Abandoning their plan to land, they climbed instead in a steep turn. They flew past the trawler, which was once again altering its bearing.

The helicopter came in low, like a dragonfly skimming the waves, and hovered noisily above the dinghy. Captain Khan's heart leapt the moment he saw the boys. Tears sprang to his eyes when he spotted Aditya waving joyously up at him. Blinking, he rose and crossed to a hatch at the rear of the machine. Unlocking it, he opened it and let down a rope.

One by one, the boys and Kumar were winched into the helicopter. Tears spilled from Captain Khan's eyes and streaked into his beard when he held Aditya, crushing him to his chest.

The dinghy was left abandoned in the sea. Captain Khan assured them that the navy would collect it later.

The helicopter rose skyward and the dinghy shrank to a bubble in the water. Mr Singh banked the machine and Shaukat pointed out the twin islands of Tinakara and Pitti. While Aditya chatted animatedly with his father, Vikram and Shaukat linked arms and gazed fondly at the islands as they fell behind them and slipped under the horizon.

The next few days were tumultuous.

Faisal's father flew down from Kalpeni to meet the boys. Shaukat was reunited with his parents. The militants and Basheer Koya and all his men were captured. Captain Khan had radioed the naval base during the return flight and within hours, naval gunboats had reached the twin islands. All were taken to Cochin and incarcerated in the jail there. Muthu and Mammen were arrested at Kadmat. So ended the kidnapping saga of Mr Kumar.

After a breathless day in Kalpeni, they all left for Kadmat. A grand reception awaited them there. Indebted to the boys for having rescued Kumar, the navy had arranged a gala function to felicitate them. Senior officers flew in from Kochi to attend. Everybody who mattered was present: the administrator, the collector, the superintendent of police and the naval chief.

Shaukat was the star of the show. His shy, deprecating demeanour notwithstanding, everyone knew that it was Shaukat who had saved the boys and was responsible for their safe return. Kumar's gratitude was boundless. He promised Shaukat a bigger and better boat than the *Alisha*. To the boys, he promised a windsurf board each.

The friends spent a few days together on Kadmat. But soon it was time for farewells. Although it wasn't even a month since Vikram and Aditya had met Faisal and Shaukat, it was as if they had known the islanders all their lives. Goodbyes were difficult. Faisal and Shaukat promised to visit the boys at their school.

And so, Vikram and Aditya departed the coral islands. For the last time, the turquoise waters and coral flashed by, and the ocean, wrinkled and tipped with froth, stretched beneath them. Somewhere in the blue world below swam a turtle. Vikram had barely spent a few hours with the creature, yet he would remember it for the rest of his life and would forever be grateful to it.

ABOUT VOLCANIC
ISLANDS AND CORALS

J ust as we have volcanoes on land, there are volcanoes that erupt under the sea. They are not particularly choosy as to whether they crop up on land or under the sea. They materialize where there is a fault in the earth's crust. Underwater eruptions have been taking place long before man arrived on Earth, but it is only now that we have started detecting and observing them.

Eruptions that take place a 1000 metres below sea level are not as spectacular as those on land. Hot, fiery magma oozes out of the earth's crust. It rapidly cools and solidifies when it comes into contact with the water around it. The volcanic material gathers in a huge heap around the deep-sea vent. Over the years, more and more material is deposited and an underwater mountain is formed. Like volcanoes on land, the undersea ones do not erupt regularly. There are periods of intense activity followed by long periods of dormancy. As the years pass—many, many thousands of them—the mountain slowly inches upwards and finally one day, it breaks the surface of the sea and an island is born.

But life is not easy for the island. The sea thunders across it, snatching away the volcanic material. The rain, too, erodes its surface and washes the island away. As long as the volcano is active, more and more material rises to the surface and the island rises out of the sea. The most famous example of a volcanic island is the Polynesian island of Hawaii, where the volcano that powered its birth is still active. Mauna Kea, as the mountain is known, has risen 4200 metres above sea level and it is still rising.

What happens when the volcano dies? Well, the sea does not forgive the intruder that has risen in its midst. It eats away at the island, gnawing and chewing at it. The rain causes mudslides and washes the mountains away. Most volcanic islands, especially those located in areas where there is plenty of rain, are doomed to die. However, there are volcanic islands that, though they should have disappeared a long time ago, somehow still exist. The secret of their survival is a marine organism. An organism that starts life as a tiny single-celled entity but eventually grows into a complex, tangled, immensely strong protective wall. That marine organism is coral.

Coral flourishes in warm, clear and shallow water, where plenty of sunlight penetrates through to the seabed. Volcanic islands, located near the equator or in the tropics, provide just the right conditions for coral.

Most people think that coral is a type of marine plant. Coral, after all, is stationary and immobile. It does grow like a plant, rooted to the ground. But despite these similar physical characteristics, coral is not a marine plant like seagrass and seaweed. Coral is of animal origin. It starts life as a tiny pinhead-sized organism. Unlike the later stages of its life when it becomes a hard immobile organism, the young coral is mobile. It is mostly carried by the flow of the ocean waters and yes, it can swim a wee bit. When the young coral encounters the shore of a volcanic island, it attaches itself to a suitable spot. Once the animal has attached itself, it can no longer move again.

The coral now begins to grow. A single coral polyp buds to give two polyps, which bud to give four and so on. The coral develops a hard skeleton, as hard as human bone, and it remains strong and unbreakable even after it dies. Coral grows in layers, with new coral growing on the dead skeleton of the old. When this process of coral growing on coral continues for hundreds of years, a wall of coral, or a reef, is formed. The most famous and spectacular coral reefs are found along the north-east coast of Australia, comprising the Great Barrier Reef.

The most precious resource of a coral island is its coral. But coral is extremely sensitive. Indiscriminate blasting or pollution can kill it. Trophy hunters who pick away at its reefs to decorate their homes can destroy its fragile ecosystem. Once coral dies, not only do the wonderful fish that inhabit its reefs die but also the island that it has protected over the centuries is doomed. The unforgiving sea, no longer hindered by a strong living barrier, surges across the island. It washes its surface away and submerges the island forever under its vast expanse.

READ MORE IN THE SERIES

Ladakh Adventure

On their visit to the Changthang plateau of Ladakh, Vikram and Aditya find themselves on the run along with Tsering, a young Tibetan boy they meet while camping on this grand yet barren frontier of India. Determined to protect Tsering from the mysterious band of men chasing him, the three boys traverse the majestic land beyond the Himalayas in search of answers.

Who is Tsering? Why is he being hunted with such fierce resolve? Follow Vikram and Aditya across the remote frozen plateau to the mountain city of Leh—through a land of startling contrasts and magnificent mountains—as a perilous game of hide-and-seek unfolds.

Journey to the roof of the world with an enthralling tale set in one of India's most splendid destinations.

READ MORE IN THE SERIES

Snow Leopard Adventure

Ages 13 and up

Vikram and Aditya are back in magnificent Ladakh. Having finally freed their young friend Tsering from the hands of dangerous men, they've set themselves up for an even greater challenge: to track down the grey ghost of the Himalayas, the snow leopard. The boys join a team of ecologists and explorers in their search for this rare and beautiful creature.

Here, Vikram befriends a troubled and unhappy girl called Caroline. The soaring peaks of the Himalayas hold no attraction for her, yet she is driven by an overpowering desire to spot a snow leopard. Set amidst majestic mountains and plunging valleys, *Snow Leopard Adventure* is a satisfying finale to a chase that began in *Ladakh Adventure*.

Journey in search of the elusive snow leopard with an enthralling tale set in one of India's most splendid destinations.